T0157592

Marceau O'Neill's

IF NOT HONOUR

A Case Against a Democratized America

iUniverse, Inc.
New York   Bloomington

If Not Honour
A Case Against a Democratized America

Copyright © 2010 Marceau O'Neill

All rights reserved. No part of this book may be used or reproduced by any means, graphic, electronic, or mechanical, including photocopying, recording, taping or by any information storage retrieval system without the written permission of the publisher except in the case of brief quotations embodied in critical articles and reviews.

This is a work of fiction. All of the characters, names, incidents, organizations, and dialogue in this novel are either the products of the author's imagination or are used fictitiously.

iUniverse books may be ordered through booksellers or by contacting:

iUniverse
1663 Liberty Drive
Bloomington, IN 47403
www.iuniverse.com
1-800-Authors (1-800-288-4677)

Because of the dynamic nature of the Internet, any Web addresses or links contained in this book may have changed since publication and may no longer be valid. The views expressed in this work are solely those of the author and do not necessarily reflect the views of the publisher, and the publisher hereby disclaims any responsibility for them.

ISBN: 978-1-4502-5167-9 (pbk)
ISBN: 978-1-4502-5169-3 (cloth)
ISBN: 978-1-4502-5168-6 (ebk)

Printed in the United States of America

iUniverse rev. date: 10/7/2010

To those who honour
individual dignity and the
traditional values which forge it.

"It cannot be doubted that in the United States the instruction of the people powerfully contributes to the support of the democratic republic; and such must always be the case, I believe, where the instruction which enlightens the understanding is not separated from the moral education..."

~Tocqueville's *Democracy In America*

Prologue

*This is a fictional projection into the future of
a once strong and self-reliant people.*

*Throughout the early Nineteenth Century up to this
story's present day, the profoundly unifying principles
of their shining republic were, with insidious cunning,
systematically deconstructed. Today, these formerly
exceptional people stand no more. Instead, they may be
found quivering, without voice, on democratized knees.*

*Our main character is a self-made professional of
extraordinary grit. Obstinately refusing to kneel
before those responsible for the gutting of her beloved
country, her behavior has been officially declared
suspect, and her classification adjudged "Remnant."*

*Dr. Brons has survived a lifetime of Distrito censure
for stubbornly disseminating her beliefs. After
decades of suffocating restrictions, this bone-weary
centenarian now questions how much longer she can
travel her chosen, increasingly dangerous, path.*

The prolonged ordeal came dangerously close to breaking her.

I
PEOPLE'S HALL, 33 ATT

She steps confidently onto the awaiting podium. Squaring to face the audience, she is instantly enveloped in a blinding light of accusatory glare. Despite her years, the woman's proud bearing is both formidable and strikingly attractive. The attendees sit motionless, watching her with apparent distaste. It is her norm to appear without Customary Concealment, so she is not bothered. As her intelligent hazel eyes carefully scan those before her, she replays the long-ago process without which today's appearance would not have been permitted.

It was in the summer of her 41st year that the BCI agent paid her an unannounced visit. Her heart still gasped in horror, recalling his cold, intimidating glare. She remembered silently praying for sustaining courage as his dark, unseeing eyes seemed to paralyze her, when she suddenly felt him thrust a paper of some sort at her and then leave as abruptly as he had arrived. Feeling fairly certain that he was actually gone, she turned her eyes to the document. It read, "Mandate to Appear." The charge cited on the next line was "Callous Disregard for the General Welfare of People's Sector 31".

The following morning, the Doctor punctually reported to the designated Tribunal cell. Having expected only the brief inconvenience of an initial hearing, she was badly shaken when a stocky deputy magistrate clasped her upper arm and dragged her into tribunal custody. Being completely unprepared to give testimony, the answers she gave in her own defense were clumsy and seemed to worsen the odds which had, apparently, been well stacked against her. There were days when she thought the trial would never end. Over a grueling seven months and five contiguous days, her persistent objections and citations of mitigating Distrito law so frustrated the Presiding Magistrate that he finally countered with threat of irreversible Distrito Censure. Had such permanent censure been invoked, she would have been subjected to indefinite containment in some remote Beneficent Care Facility. The sustained cruelties imposed by redemption procedures in those facilities could only be imagined.

The tribunal's anonymous witness had accused the Doctor of violating People's Mandate 617. The all-encompassing Global Regulatory Advisement was cited as the governing authority. 617 violations proscribed any and all manner of insensitive expression. They were customarily reported by way of the easy-to-access Peoples' Victimization Link and required no confirming identification of the accuser. Adding to the Doctor's dismay, there had been no specifics cited to describe her alleged offense. Under the Link report's "Resultant Injuries" column, an innocuous-looking "X" appeared across from "Insensitivities Suffered." In practice, the mere accusation of such vile behavior was all that was needed to instantly trigger an automated demand that an accused appear.

The prolonged ordeal came dangerously close to breaking her. Unable to prove her innocence, the Doctor was eventually deemed guilty of the alleged crime. Astonishingly, however, a codified Special Need saved her from mandatory containment. It was explained by the magistrate that her Remnant classification clearly entitled her to certain lawful protection given the disabled and, as such, GRA provisions stipulated tribunal clemency. The Doctor could barely contain her joy as the magistrate announced his decision to waive sentencing. He closed with a caveat that tribunal clemency was entirely contingent upon her maintaining a current Remnant permit that provided the requisite disclosure of her deviant status.

Throughout the ensuing years, those permit renewals were swiftly processed. More recently, however, they had become increasingly more restrictive and carried punishing penalties. The most recent renewal, which allowed today's public lecture, had been processed only hours before she was scheduled to speak. Its term had been severely reduced to a scant seventy-two hours and issuance predicated upon the advance posting of a 50-unit compliance bond. She was well aware that today's permit also carried a microscopic footnote of warning. Displayed in regulation font size 6, it threatened closed-end containment in the event even one more complaint "of any scope" came to be lodged against her.

From the raised platform, the Doctor calmly looked into her audience, recognizing how grotesque her appearance must be. Interestingly, the younger ones seemed to be eyeing her with curiosity, rather than the usual disgust. Standing proudly before them, she breathed in deeply and thought, *"I know, just know, that this time someone will hear me."*

~~~

"Daddy's home!" she whispered excitedly.

II
CHICAGO NORTHSIDE, 1948 AD

The child winced, as her tiny bare toes touched the bone-chilling asbestos tiles. Her feet instantly recoiled to the security beneath her warm woolen blankets. She was sure she had heard them talking and simply had to watch. Resolutely, she stretched her toes a second time to reach the freezing floor below. Whimpering soundlessly, she placed both feet onto the sub-zero tile and tiptoed quietly to the curtained doors.

The haunting melody wafted from the dining room. Shivering not so much from the cold, but from the fear of what she was certain to witness, the four-year-old timidly reached for the delicate lace curtains. As she drew them aside with the tips of her chilled little fingers, she thought, "Really, really careful, now... They mustn't know I'm watching."

She peeked through the diamond-shaped glass pane and glimpsed a reassuring scene of her mother at the old mahogany upright. A bare light bulb hung from fraying ceiling wires, shedding a meager glow onto the scene below. Comforted to see her mother's luxurious auburn mane nestled about her firm, squared shoulders, the four-year-old breathed a soft sigh of relief. Stifling a sleepy yawn, her innocent eyes followed those graceful fingers glide deftly along the chipped ivory keys.

"I thought that love was over, that we were really through…" Her mother's sweet soprano voice sang out haltingly, between sobs. Then came that rich baritone harmony: "I said I don't love her, that we'd begin anew…" As the child blinked to clear her very blue, very sleepy eyes, she saw from the corner of her fragmented view a familiar, beautifully strong, sinewed hand reaching down to her mother. Recognizing immediately what was about to happen, little Aly felt the usual compulsion to run away, back to the safety of her warm bed. But, just as quickly, she decided to remain. Unconsciously bracing herself, she recalled dreamily, "When they dance, it's sooooo pretty!"

Her beautiful mother's eyes were swollen and looked pleadingly beyond the outstretched hand. "And you can all believe me, we sure intended to," she sang with him between stifled sobs. Although his face was outside of the child's vision, she knew that the beckoning hand was her father's. "Daddy's home!" she whispered excitedly. Now completely reassured, she closed her delicate lids and squeezed them tightly to better savor the richness of her father's hypnotic croon.

"But, we just couldn't say goodbye." Just as she began opening her bright hazel eyes, Aly saw her mother rise from the safety of the wooden piano bench and cautiously step toward the powerful *arms awaiting her. As she watched her mother's tear-drenched face and fearful eyes, she was reminded of a trapped fawn, pitiful and frightened. Sobbing woefully, her mother resigned herself to those outstretched arms poised to encircle her.*

The pair was moving into full view of their unseen intruder. "Oh! How I love this part! Mommy and Daddy look so happy when they dance!" mouthed the blonde child happily. She opened her eyes widely, to make sure not to miss a thing. "The chair and then the sofa, they broke right down and cried..." She nodded approvingly, as her mother and father slowly swayed to their special tune. Daddy's rich baritone voice crooned ever so softly in Mommy's ear: "The curtain started parting for me to come inside." Aly loved the sweetness of her mommy's harmony, although now wretchedly muffled. "How beautiful," she thought. "Mommy and daddy love each other so much!"

Within a split second, the child's reverie shattered. "Please, Kurt, no!" her mother whimpered. Then, the all-too-familiar sight; her father's muscular arm drew back, and then struck forcibly against his wife's already bruised cheekbone.

"Why do you always have to ruin things?" he growled. His arms tightened about his now cringing dance partner. "Stop crying!" he hissed between clenched teeth. "Besides," he quickly countered, "I didn't hit you all that hard!" This he whispered against the now swollen, freshly welted cheek. The couple continued their shuffling dance steps. "I tell you confidentially, the tears were hard to hide..." Tears seemed to pour from the reddened rims

of her mother's frightened eyes. She remained wary with face downward, tightly restrained by her husband's arms. Such helplessness frightened Aly and tugged at her little innocent heart. "Why does it always end this way?" the child asked herself. With great caution she slowly released curtains from her chilled, tightly clenched fist. She held still for a moment and listened quietly. Once satisfied that she had not been discovered, she quietly tiptoed toward the security of her beckoning single cot, being very careful not to awaken her youngest brother, who slept undisturbed nearby. Noiselessly, she slid gingerly beneath her wool blanket of cardinal red-and-black Scotch plaid. She felt relieved, but took great care to remain silent.

In the distance, she heard, "No, Kurt! Please don't!" Then came the "c-r-a-c-k" Aly had grown to recognize. "More ugly bumps on Mommy's face tomorrow, that's for sure!" she affirmed innocently with a quickly nodding head. Now the heart-breaking whimpering, wretched and mournful. "I'll just go back to sleep really fast, so everything'll be OK," the child reassured herself. She closed her eyelids tightly and willed herself to safety. It only took a millisecond for Aly to expediently transport herself. Sliding deeper and deeper into her self-created stronghold, she continued to hear, "… that we just couldn't say 'goodbye'." The haunting duet grew fainter and fainter until she heard it no more. Smiling, little Aly nestled into the consoling cushion of soothing silence.

~~~

"That's anti-Distrito talk, isn't it?"

III
PEOPLE'S HALL, 09:42

The auditorium was massive and its bare austerity unsettling. "With the permission of our Sector, I am here to speak to you as a Remnant," the old woman announced. "By pure definition, a Remnant believes that no one, not even our all-governing Sector, has the moral right to provide for them." Among the sea of vacant stares, she noticed a sprinkling of puzzlement. She smiled kindly. "I see you may have questions." Nodding slightly toward the front row, she asked, "You, Ciudadano, do you wish clarification of my statement?"

A gaunt-looking male, shamefully displaying excessive height, rose timidly to his feet. In spite of the obvious alterations to his face, she estimated his chronological age to be between 45 and 50 calendar years. It had been nearly 40 years ago when Peoples' Rights legislation was expanded to proscribe certain offending DNA properties. Immediately thereafter, pre-cloning measures were implemented. Also, any citizen who had the misfortune of displaying even one of the outlawed characteristics and/or had been born prior to the date of that retroactive mandate was legally compelled to submit to remedial correction. This man's precision-sculpted bone structure and flawless complexion were the conspicuous results of such correction. He was, indeed, a handsome fellow, she thought, even though his perfectly chiseled features were strangely devoid of expression. This starkly contrasted his body language, which exhibited a disturbing hint of agitation.

The speaker was somehow intrigued by the man's highly polished cranium, which swiveled searchingly from side to side. Upon sighting the primary feed just below the podium, he steadied his stance. She guessed that this was for his optimal transmission. "I am Waters of Sector 31," he announced. "Why aren't you communicating with DI?"

"Thank you for your candor, Sir," she replied cheerfully. "As I trust you will appreciate, being a true Remnant, I am not physically equipped to communicate by the Direct Interface medium. From the represented ages of this audience, I'll assume that no one here today is physiologically capable of communicating by way of their auditory and oral senses, as am I. You see," she added hurriedly, "I was born decades before DI technology was routinely adopted and, because my advanced age renders me socially unsuitable for implementation, the Sector has excused me from undergoing surgical alterations required for that modality. To be more responsive to your question, however, and for the benefit of those of you who are unfamiliar with this matter, please allow me to briefly explain the mechanics of how we will be communicating today."

"In compliance with Altruistic Law, this public facility is DI-adaptive. Direct Interface is a technology that acts as a conduit between communicators; one citizen's brain transmits its message and that message is instantaneously received by the recipient citizen's brain. This is a commonplace genetic birthright that most, or all of you, were provided immediately upon conception. Because I am without that genetic enhancement, I continue to communicate verbally, through the action of my mouth, tongue, vocal chords, and so on. (Please see me after the lecture if you'd like more details about this.) So, in order for me to "hear" the words you think to me, they are intercepted by the DI adaptors in this auditorium, then scanned, translated, and transmitted audibly into this room in my preferred language. Furthermore, because I am not physically endowed with DI, when I speak to you, as I am doing now, my vocalized words are being instantly translated by and transmitted to you via DI. To sum this up, your communications will be projected to me audibly with basic, antiquated sound waves and mine will be digitally transmitted directly to your cerebral receptors. While Altruistic regulation requires these accommodations, I truly hope that my facial animations today, which are necessary to vocalization, do not become an affront to your sensibilities."

Within the periphery of her vision, the Doctor saw the tall man, eyes downcast, lowering himself back into his seat. "Mister Waters," she quickly called to him, "did you have another question?" With a promising glint of recognition and seemingly great effort, he returned to a standing position. "Yes, Doctor. It troubles me that you said something earlier about your kind – Remnants – don't believe our Sector has the moral right to provide for them." That's anti-Distrito talk, isn't it?"

She sensed mounting tension and could hear faint sounds of unrest. Bracing herself, she took one purposeful step forward, and announced: "Good people! I humbly ask your patience for only a moment, while I attempt to answer Mister Water's question. Please show us the courtesy of your attention."

Dr. Brons stood with proud conviction, posture boldly erect. "Yes, you do understand me correctly, Mister Waters. Being a Remnant," she continued, "I come from a time when self-reliance was diligently instilled in children during their formative years. At that time, this independent strength was considered a virtue by a society, and was deemed a highly regarded characteristic of mature, responsible adults. As was then customary, self-reliance was initially taught to me by my mother and father, who raised me to understand that conducting one's life with dignified autonomy was the only acceptable way to live." As she had anticipated, her words were not being at all well received. In spite of the waves of disapproving murmurs, though, the old woman pursued her speaking rhythm. She knew it was absolutely crucial – today of all days – to cover every bit of material she had come to present.

"During my youth, offspring were nurtured lovingly as 'children' and each child was generally reared by both a father, the male, and a mother, the female, in a shared home. These mothers and fathers were called 'parents' and they had the primary responsibility of raising their own biologically-produced offspring. Such 'raising' not only equipped the children with the basic skills needed to engage in formal schooling, but also included the teaching of acceptable societal and cultural concepts to which they were expected to adhere. The primary concepts of which I speak were self-discipline, self-reliance, and self-accountability."

What had been inscrutable silence was now deteriorating into unrest. It was utterly surreal, she thought, to see all those lips turning pallid, as they drew tightly over voiceless mouths. Entranced, she felt the room pulsate with digitized bleats of, "Untrue! Untrue! Distrito will not tolerate untruths! "

~~~

*"Come in, Child," she told her, pushing
open the weather-beaten door...*

IV
EAST LOS ANGELES, 1949 AD

It was a typically overcast morning. Six-year-old Aly didn't mind the heat, though, as she skipped along Vermont Avenue toward the neighborhood five-and-dime. Her grandmother was in the process of making some awfully pretty school ribbons for her braids, but found there wasn't enough material for both golden tresses. So, Grandma had entrusted Aly with the "goodly sum of two bits" to go buy the needed length of Scotch plaid taffeta.

She felt like such a grownup! With shoulders back, Aly proudly entered the store all by herself. She approached the kindly Mr. Spiegel with the same confidence Grandma had when she allowed her to run this solo errand. Looking up to his eyes, she gleefully handed him the scrap of paper from her grandmother. On it was a detailed description of the ribbon she wanted the child to buy.

Mr. Spiegel looked down warmly at Aly over the tops of his delicately gold-rimmed bifocals. Stooping down to her, he spoke his customary greeting: "Good morning, Fraulein Aly. So, you und deine Grossmutter again make Schulkleider, ja?" As she met the gaze of his soft brown eyes, Aly nodded demurely, and then mimicked his shuffle, following him to the yardage table near the back wall. Against wallpapered images of bright yellow daffodils and snowy strawberry blossoms, she watched the wizened old storekeeper intently, as he rolled out the gigantic wheel of ribbon from the overhead bin. As the ribbon unfurled, little Aly was enthralled by the endless flow of the prettiest, shiniest, ribbon she had ever seen. Mr. Spiegel counted, "Ein Fuss, zwei, vier, und... ja...sechs!" "Das ist alles, Kleinchen!" Aly gave out her usual titter at hearing his funny sounding speech. He held up two yards of crisp taffeta ribbon along side her heat-flushed cheek and said, "Soon you vill be varink dies wunderschoenes ribbon, Kleinchen!" She nodded excitedly, her wide hazel eyes never leaving his freshly shaven, sagging face. As the storeowner handed her a small paper bag containing the precious purchase, he asked, "Du hast eight cents in change, Child, enough to buy five Pfeffermint candies, yes?" Without hesitation, Aly quickly replied, "No, Sir, Gramma wants me to buy the ribbon and that's all." With twinkling eyes, he gently placed the bright copper pennies onto her small, outstretched palm. The six-year-old raced out the screened door, shouting an exuberant "Thank you, Mr. Pseegel!" The storeowner waved heartily, watching his favorite little patron slowly submerge into the undulating pedestrian flow.

Minutes later, Aly returned to her grandmother's front porch. She politely tapped her little knuckles three times on the doorframe and waited. "Is that you, Aly?" a melodious voice called out.

"Yes, Gramma," she answered, looking up expectantly into the darkness beyond the screen.

"Come in, Child," she told her, pushing open the weather-beaten door for her granddaughter to enter, the rusted springs screeching in familiar protest. Having completed the mission assigned her, Aly stepped inside with pronounced deliberation, her nostrils delighting in the alluring aroma of baking rhubarb pies.

"Did Mr. Spiegel have the ribbon we wanted?" the woman asked. Wordlessly, Aly proudly held up the crinkly brown paper bag to her grandmother. "Thank you, Little One," said the woman, reaching for the prize. As though in slow motion, Grandma O'Rourke carefully peeked inside the small bag, her soft Gaelic blues wide with playful expectation. Ever so slowly the old woman inched the snaking ribbon from the bag, lifting it to the afternoon sunlight for inspection. Aly watched, stoically awaiting her grandmother's edict. "Yes!" the woman proclaimed. "This is exactly what we want for Aly's school braids!" Then, with playful solemnity and brows slowly rising, "And the change, Young Lady?"

Their gazes locked playfully. Aly reached into the paper bag, her little fingers seeking out the coins Mr. Spiegel had entrusted to her. Once they were all in her grasp, she swiftly pulled them from the bag, and ceremoniously splayed them in her upturned palm. Her grandmother's eyes flitted quickly from coin to coin and then ever so slowly returned Aly's hopeful gaze. Placing her left hand firmly beneath the child's outstretched hand, her right hand plucked up the Indian Head nickel and three well-worn copper pennies. A *wide, approving smile shone on the woman's face. "Such a lovely one you are, Child! We can always count on Aly to do the grownup thing. 'Send you out to buy something, and you always come back with exactly what Gram asked for, and – you little dickens you – you always manage to bring back change! Now your brothers… well, that's a different story!"*

Grandma O'Rourke pulled her granddaughter to her, firmly planting a playful smooch on the youngster's cheek. The reassurance of it all filled the child with joy. "Right now, your mother is getting home from work and probably needs your help with dinner." She opened the rusty screeching door, and snapped her terry cloth apron playfully at the child's bottom. "Now, off with you! Tomorrow we'll braid your hair and put on those lovely ribbons you bought. " The joy of her grandmother's expressed approval filled Aly near to bursting. Smiling widely from ear to ear, she bounded down the rickety porch steps. Humming with self-approval, she ran hurriedly across the rustic courtyard toward home.

As she ran joyfully toward the weathered clapboard rental, Aly squealed happily, "Grandma says I did a good job! Mommy likes how good I do things for her, too." Her confidence well fortified, the child ran into the small wooden house to find her mother. "Mommy, are you home?" Her eyes searched anxiously about the cramped kitchen area. Almost immediately she located her mother sitting at their shiny, new chrome-Formica table. "Mommy's my very own beautiful angel," Aly thought dreamily. As she awaited her mother's greeting, she decided she was ready to take on whatever dinner time chore her mother asked of her. Whatever it might be, she would be good, not complain, and do it well.

Leaning against the white enamel O'Keefe & Merritt, Aly watched her mother as she counted her tips from the early morning shift. First the quarters: "Two, four, one dollar; two, four, two dollars; two, four, three dollars". Then the dimes: "Two, four, six, eight, ten, one dollar; two, four six, eight, ten, two dollars..." On and on she counted, carefully setting up neat stacks on the grey-specked kitchen table. "Some day I'll go to work like you, Mommy. I'll bring home lots and lotsa money, so I can take care of you."

Margaret's busy fingers continued their rhythmic sweep of one coin after the other into their one-dollar piles. She looked up appreciatively at her daughter and said, "Thank you, my little princess. I know you will. But, for right now, Mommy wants you to help her by putting these stacks of coins into the piggy bank, so she can get dinner ready. Aly dutifully did as her mother asked. With solemn precision, she deposited the tallied coins into the jelly jar's crudely slotted lid. Her mother was saving her meager, hard-earned tips to purchase the next household item they didn't have, but very much needed, just like the pretty Formica table at which they now sat and the family gathered for meals. Her mommy made certain that each such purchase was yet another surprise for her children. As though leading a royal procession, the five-year-old ceremoniously carried the money jar to her mother's bedroom. With the utmost ado, she solemnly hid it in their secret place.

Two hours latter, Aly was standing beside her three barefoot brothers. The foursome was waving in unison to their mother, who was hurrying to catch the street car that would take her back to the café for the second shift that day. The four youngsters watched her as she cautiously negotiated the steep, crumbling driveway to the boulevard stop below. With each carefully placed step, Margaret O'Rourke gradually disappeared from view; first, her shapely, athletic legs, and then those well-toned arms and shoulders, until her image was lost but for their memories.

~~~

"Take her! Take her away!"

V

PEOPLE'S HALL, 11:17

The silence was deafening to the Doctor's ears. Drawing strength from past memory, she inhaled and exhaled slowly, with controlled, reviving breaths. "My mother's people were considered 'Shanty Irish'." A collective gasp instantly shot throughout the hall. As the DI transmitter thrust forth a simulated screech from her mute audience, the old woman's regal countenance was unflinching. "Her people," she continued, "immigrated to America in full observance of and compliance with the then-laws of the land." Hostility seemed to permeate the air. "My mother's family came to this continent with no expectation other than the then-laudable premise of accomplishment earned by hard work." Rhythmic shouts pulsated from the overhead, "Take her! Take her away! Her words are hateful and no son permitidas!"

"As *legal* immigrants, my mother's family understood that this country extended to them only two guarantees; the first, that the merit of their work ethic would be rewarded by capitalistic prosperity, according to the quality and constancy of that hard work, and the second, each individual would be judged according to his own merit."

Utter pandemonium broke out. A wave of threatening fists shook mightily, as their owners jumped out of their seats in angry protest. The uproar was deafening. The Behavioral Compliance Officer assigned to People's Hall that day scurried angrily up the center aisle and onto the stage, deftly positioning himself between the audience and the speaker. He glared menacingly at the Doctor, as he raised his arm agitatedly toward the protesters, his face-out palm commanding their silence. As the protests began to quell, the Doctor's ears heard the welcomed sound of her father's call: *"Aly! Peter!"*

~~~

"Come on, Kids, let's go for a ride!"

VI
FAREWELL, EL SEGUNDO, 1950 AD

Aly and Peter worked feverishly to reinforce their newest escape tunnel. They had to move fast, so they'd finish before they were called in for dinner.

During school vacations, this was their most favorite place. It was magical here, where they could spend uninterrupted hours playing under the hot Pacific Coast sun, delicious ocean breeze, and gusty salt air. This summer day was pretty much like all the others they had come to take for granted. While hurrying to shore up the newer tunnel wall, they were serenaded by incessant squawks of sea gulls and the thunder of crashing waves. According to his custom, Peter never missed a chance to taunt his little sister. At this moment, he was in hiding outside the tunnel entrance, giggling soundlessly, as she called and called to him from inside. Aly was desperate to have Peter check her work before they had to go in for the day.

Above the clamor of ocean noises, they suddenly heard the sharp commanding voice. "Peter! Aly! Come on out and get over here!"

Climbing to the top of their tunneled dune, they both turned toward the masculine voice and were startled to see a vaguely familiar-looking man in the distance. He was waving excitedly to them, as he leaned ostentatiously against a big, shiny black car. It was strangely reassuring to see the half-smoked Camel clenched tensely between his teeth. That picture, coupled with his tan windbreaker and sweat-stained hat brim, gave way to instant remembering. "Could it really be?" they thought in disbelief. Transfixed, their bewildered eyes also recognized Patrick and Paulie, who stood timidly at the man's side.

"Come on, Kids, let's go for a ride!" he shouted over the pounding waves. In less than a flash, the two youngsters exchanged consenting glances, grinning with glee. "It's Daddy!" they squealed excitedly, racing to be the first to reach their father's beckoning arms.

Aly and Peter ran as fast as their young legs would carry them. Kurt smiled widely, flashing his even white teeth and engaging dimpled cheeks. He scooped up his youngest two and hugged them tightly. With each child now nestled contentedly in a well-muscled arm, the young father beamed with joy. "Guess what? We're going for a fun ride today!" he announced, smiling.

"OK, but first we have to ask Mommy," they chimed happily.

"Daddy's already taken care of that, and it's OK," he said reassuringly. "Besides, this ride is on your mother," he added solemnly, setting the two down at an opened rear car door. Golly,

*what a grand day it had become, actually seeing their daddy
again!*

*Aly and Peter dove into the back seat, their happy hearts near to
bursting. Aly half-heartedly glimpsed her two older brothers, who
were already seated in the back. Patrick and Paulie were staring
blankly ahead. Neither was smiling.*

~~~

*The pressure in her ears was excruciating. Aly wanted to cry out and
plead with her daddy to make the hurt go away, but, remembered
well he did not tolerate whining. Amidst the deafening roar of
twin props, she began to whimper, but quickly checked herself.
Seeing her grimace, her father reassured her they were close to the
end of their ride. "Even though Mommy is paying for this ride,
I don't like it. It's too long and I want to go home," she thought
inwardly. She remained obediently silent, nestled submissively
in her father's strong arms. Aly was grateful for what warmth his
windbreaker provided her chilled bare arms, legs, and feet. She
had decided that, no matter how much her ears hurt, she would
bear the pain to avoid his displeasure.*

*Kurt Brons looked down at his little girl's pallid face just as it
began to pinch up. He quickly grabbed a vomit bag from his jacket
pocket and placed it firmly at her tightly contorted mouth. Aly
felt her daddy hold her securely while she groaned, leaned forward,
and spewed relief for the fifth time since takeoff.*

It seemed like an eternity before the Douglas DC-3 began its descent into Chicago's Midway Airport. As though in twilight, she heard her father telling her brothers they'd soon be getting off the plane and going to see Grandpa. Although confused, she understood that to mean she would not be going home that day. Sick, hungry, and exhausted, Aly thought of her mother setting the table for supper without her. As the plane made its approach for landing, she remained stoic, tears silently tumbling from her now frightened young eyes.

~~~

The air became stunningly still.

VII
PEOPLE'S HALL, 12:02

"Doctora! The People...they are demanding you conduct yourself en una manera aprobaba!" the BC Officer spat. The man panned the audience to reappraise its mood. Finding the attendees had reassumed a posture of curious attention, he turned back to the aged woman and locked onto her eyes with a chilling glare. "You must behave, Doctora," he hissed with disgust, then spun around and hurriedly left the platform.

"My comments seem to have distressed you," she continued speaking. "So, to preface the remainder of my presentation, I wish to call your attention to the fact that I am Distrito-authorized to speak to you of The Old Ways. We all know that grievous penalties await those who dare to whisper this unmentionable subject anywhere outside of a specifically sanctioned venue, such as this hall, and I do assure you I will do all that's reasonable to avoid such penalties. Additionally, I am well aware that The Old Ways will, quite understandably, be unsettling to some of you, and may even sound anarchic. However, I assure you that inciting anarchy is not my goal. Rather, I chose this topic purely for your intellectual enhancement. If you'll be kind enough to hear me out, you will leave here today with the ability to boast of a live accounting from a living, breathing anachronism. Something, I dare say, you will probably never again experience. Certainly, not from me!" she grinned engagingly.

"I further remind you, though, that my notorious Old Ways are what titillated your interest in the first place to attend today's presentation. So, I now caution all who wish to remain for the duration of my talk that today's topic was selected intentionally to challenge what might remain of your capacity for what was once known as 'deductive reasoning.' If you're not up for this intellectual challenge, I strongly recommend that you leave now. Should you decide to leave, you may take with you my personal guarantee of recompense for any emotional damages you believe you have suffered." The Doctor paused to scrutinize those seated in the first several rows before her. Surprised, but gratified, her offer was being met with complete and utter calm. "Very well!" she said cheerily, "let's get on with it, shall we?

"I mentioned that my mother's people were considered 'Shanty Irish' and, although never on the 'dole,' they were looked upon as undesirables. It was thought during those days that people from the Emerald Isle were shiftless parasites that hosted upon the hard-working, productive individuals, who had migrated to this land before them. It was commonly presumed, although incorrectly so, that the Irish saw themselves as victims of misfortune. On the contrary! Although throngs of Irishmen did arrive on these shores as victims of blight and famine, as a people, they wholly believed and trusted in the promise of our United States of America. They understood and held dear the promise of unfettered freedom for all individuals to pursue their own happiness."

She had no sooner completed her sentence when a number of hands shot up, waving frantically for the speaker's attention. Simultaneously, the BC module began pulsating threateningly from the back wall.

"Ah, I see that Overseer believes I have again behaved wrongly," she announced. Unmoved, she nodded toward the gaunt man who had introduced himself earlier. "Mister Waters, would you please offer an explanation of my perceived indiscretion?" The man rose without hesitation, this time with a surprising touch of confidence.

"Overseer is warning you that your untruths are crimes against The People and won't be tolerated."

"And, Ciudadano Waters," she interjected softly, "would you be so kind as to also enumerate those 'untruths' to which you refer?"

"Well, sure. First, everyone knows that that all liberated People everywhere have the right to equal consumption. I mean," he stammered, "as liberated People, we can do what we want and get distributed whatever we want, according to what we really need. We're already happy, so talking about 'pursuing happiness' is a dumb waste of our time."

"Is that your complete explanation, Ciudadano?" she inquired, holding his gaze. "Of course," he retorted smugly, reseating himself.

"Dear People, we just heard Mister Waters state the gist of current law," she announced, "and that statement explains why the BC surveillance module is now flashing its repeated warning. However, I again remind you that I am speaking today of The Old Times and, in so doing, out of necessity I must refer to the conditions and circumstances of the American belief system that existed at that time. The words I use and historical references I make may seem to some of you like falsehoods or unorthodox fantasies. I find this understandable. Nevertheless, the official Variance Certification I have been issued allows me to speak as I wish during this gathering, with almost no codified limitation whatsoever. I must insist, therefore, that said module be deactivated until my lecture has concluded."

The air became stunningly still. All heads had stopped nodding. Not one raised fist remained. The module's pulsations had actually ceased.

~~~

Daddy was saying he would come
back with blankets…

VIII
STONE PARK HIDEAWAY

Little Aly stood shivering at her father's side, comforted by the grasp of his strong, calloused, hand. As she clutched he daddy's worn linen windbreaker, she looked warily at the four walls of cold concrete blocks. How lost and confused she felt! None of this made sense. Why were they here? The boys and she were supposed to have gone for a simple car ride that afternoon and then be taken home to their mother. They all should be at their shiny new kitchen table having supper right now; not here, whatever this place was. The 6-year-old's teeth chattered and her bare feet ached horribly from the stone-cold floor. "I hope that Mommy remembers to feed my baby doll," she thought.

Aly looked haltingly about the strange, unwelcoming place, while her father whispered stern orders to the boys. Her eyes came upon an old, worn mattress leaning against the stacked boxes near the door. Daddy was saying he would come back with blankets, and was warning the boys not to touch those boxes if they knew what was good for them. She was intrigued by the tiny wooden cabinet to his right, thinking how perfectly it would fit in her friend, Suki's, playhouse back home.

"While I'm gone, it's your job to cook supper, Patrick. There's an egg and box of spaghetti in here, "he said, opening the tiny cabinet door. "And there's a hotplate over there," he added, nodding toward the utility sink's counter. Get it cooked and your brothers and little sister fed before you put them to bed."

Aly's ears perked up, realizing that her daddy was going to leave them again. He seemed pretty nervous, as he hurriedly barked orders at Patrick, emphasizing to his eldest son that he would be in charge of her and the younger boys. "Under no circumstances are any of you to leave this room. The landlords live upstairs and want it quiet. When I get back, if they tell me they heard so much as a peep out of any of you, you'll be damned sorry!" As though for good measure, Kurt Brons gave each of his children his usual intense, threateningly stare.

He kneeled down to Aly and little Peter, giving each a brisk goodbye hug. "I'm counting on you two to mind your brothers!" he said matter-of-factly, and then stood back up. Aly watched her daddy adoringly as he positioned on his balding head that familiar hat she so loved to see him wear. Saying no more, he turned from them, stepped out the door, and closed it noiselessly behind him.

Patrick quickly took charge of his younger brothers and sister with his usual efficiency. "Paulie, find a pot somewhere and fill it with water at the sink. Peter, get the spaghetti out, while I look for a place to plug in that hotplate." Aly watched admiringly as her thirteen-year-old big brother grabbed the old, soiled mattress and dragged it to the center of the room. "And you, Aly," he was saying, "ya better get those bare feet off that cold floor. Hey, I know what! Sit Indian-style on the mattress to keep yourself warm. And, Peetie, after you get the spaghetti out, get on the mattress with Aly. I want you both to stay off the floor until Dad can bring you some shoes and socks. You both might as well practice your new spelling words 'til supper's ready."

~~~

"They were expected to either be adequately self-sufficient...or...do without."

IX
PEOPLE'S HALL, 12:12

"OK! It appears that, even though you are aware that our BC warning system has been deactivated, you have opted to remain for this lecture. Please know that I appreciate your forbearance and will now continue the story of my family's immigration to this great land of opportunity. I was explaining that my family did not accept or tolerate what they referred to as "the myth of victimhood." My mother's entire family was proud – yes, I intentionally mean to say "proud"- of their individual accomplishments. My mother was parented and given twelve years of public education, which society – in those days – deemed indispensable. In addition to that educational foundation, she was schooled by her family in skills preparatory to marriage. Those skills included such accomplishments as gardening, animal husbandry, baking, cooking, cleaning, clothing construction, child rearing, and managing finances." She stopped for emphasis and looked from left to right across the room to find facial expressions ranging from wide-eyed disbelief to grimaces of disgust.

"My mother was 19 years of age when she married my father, who was 22 that year," she went on. "They had no place of their own to stay and no money to rent lodging, so, they initially relied on older family members for a small room and cooked meals."

"Why didn't they just pick up their Distrito beneficios?" a voice called out.

"Because, Ciudadano, during those times, government beneficios did not exist. And, when they were provided in later years, my parents would not have qualified. You see, due to their parents' national origin, they would not have qualified as a deserving minority. Besides, most people at that time were fiercely independent. They were expected to be either adequately self-sufficient to take care of themselves and their family members, or, quite simply, do without."

The same voice yelled out again: "Come on, Doctora, how is that possible? Distrito has never allowed anyone to do without. What you say is ...ridiculo!"

"Sir, if you do not believe what I say, kindly keep your outbreaks to yourself and allow me to finish. There will be ample opportunity for discussion when I've said what must be said. While I'm speaking, think of me solely as your entertainer, if you wish, and my story the absurd rambling of an aging Remnant. But, please be still and listen. Can you do that?" she added sternly.

"Well, sure, but you don't need to be so harsh," the man whined. The Doctor looked at him, with unmasked contempt. Checking herself, she quickly turned her back to him in an attempt to hide her disgust.

"'I have no right to be 'so harsh','" she mocked him silently. *"Give me strength!" I remember when a man would go toe-to-toe and actually debate me; not whine pathetically, like a peevish child! God Almighty, are there no real men about-anywhere?!"*

Determined not to be deterred, she went on. "As I was saying, my mother and father were ill prepared to marry, and certainly ill-equipped to responsibly raise a family. But, the cultural standards of their generation demanded individual self-reliance, something they – by virtue of marrying – had no choice but to meet."

~~~

*"Daddy, do you think Mommy
is happy in Heaven?"*

X
SWEET DREAMS, LITTLE ONE

"Don't forget to say a prayer for Mommy," Kurt Brons prompted softly. Aly obeyed by dutifully reciting that very special mention, as she knelt before the tiny wall niche that housed her cherished statuette of the Holy Virgin Mary. This was Aly's special goodnight time when she asked for things in a way which only an innocent could.

She wrapped the tiny onyx beads tightly around her unwashed hands, bowed her head devoutly, and completed the final rosary for that day. "And, please Holy Mother of Baby Jesus, take good care of Mommy in Heaven. Amen." She felt pleased to have fulfilled her final duty of the day. She crossed herself in reverence, taking a stealthy sideways peek at her daddy.

Kurt Brons was kneeling in prayer beside her. Knowing his little girl was hoping for some sign of his approval, he nodded and whispered softly, "That's my girl. The Holy Mother will be sure to watch over your mommy now." Then, as was now their nightly ritual, they both rose simultaneously from their kneeling positions on the old linoleum floor. With his hand placed reassuringly on his daughter's shoulder, he guided her gently to bed.

Aly understood that, because she was a girl, she was given the very special privilege of her very own Army cot in the privacy of her very own bedroom, while her brothers and father shared two small double beds off the kitchen. This was the most special time of her day. As she slipped beneath the security of two Army-issue woolen blankets, Aly's father kissed her forehead tenderly. "Sweet dreams, Little One," he said softly, tucking her in.

Aly suddenly reached up and locked her little arms tightly about her daddy's strong neck. Looking into his eyes solemnly, she asked, "Daddy, do you think Mommy is happy in Heaven?" Returning her embrace, he replied, "You just keep praying, Al', and Mommy will be just fine." Satisfied with his assurance, the child relaxed her arms and lay back onto the faded striped mattress. Her daddy blew out the candle and quietly left the room. She smiled. Never had a child been as thrilled as she to have a vacated, musty clothes closet to call their very own. It was a quiet place, where she could live whatever dream she wished. Falling softly into slumber, Aly relished her feelings of comfort. The delicious sea breeze now caressed her face, as she raced to sun-warmed dunes and beckoning castles of sand.

~~~

"What a stupid little mouse," she thought.

XI
PEOPLE'S HALL, 13:01

"Initially, they stayed in a relative's cold-water flat. After awhile, my father found work and was able to pay for a place of their own."

"Why are you telling us this garbage?" It was the whiner again. "We all have better things to do than listen to this crazy talk! At least, I know *I* do! You may think you're entertaining us, but I sure as hell don't! All this stuff is a bunch of lies; just lies from someone too ancient to even be allowed in this Hall."

"What a stupid little mouse," she thought. "How I'd like to shake some sense into his ignorant head!"

"Enough!" she shouted. "If, Sir, I am, as you say, 'too ancient' to be allowed here, then how do you explain the fact that I am, indeed, actually here?" she added with exasperation. "Listen, everybody!" she called out. "I've already duly disclosed to this audience that my speaking topic has been officially permitted and, because of that, I am here, standing before you. That very fact, Sir, in and of itself, belies your statement. "

"Well, yeah. But, so what?" he countered feebly.

"With all the 'due' respect I'm able to muster for you right now, Sir, I must say you argue like a child. I am simply making the point that, if you have an opinion, please state it and qualify it as such, rather than making false statements. I caution you that to proclaim that what I say is 'a bunch of lies' is inherently incorrect, for I have empirical evidence to the contrary. So you see, if I were 'too old to be allowed in this Hall,' el Distrito would have disallowed my application to present to you today. So, if you disagree with what I have just said, please so stipulate by..."

"Damn! There you go again!" he interrupted.

"'Go again'? What do you mean I 'go again'?" she asked, now a bit amused.

"You know what I mean!" he ranted. "Besides lying, you talk all hoity toity, like you think yer better than us – better than me!"

This took her aback. "I beg your pardon, Sir?"

"See? There you go again! He cried shrilly. "You can't call me 'Sir'! And, all those big words! Why don't you just lower yourself enough to talk plain, like the rest of us?"

"That is simply preposterous!" she blurted out. You may believe my words are 'big' and I concur that they are more expressive than those you choose to exercise. However, I carefully select my words to adequately convey my thoughts. If I were to use your vocabulary, rather than mine, I believe that would show disrespect to you," she added softly.

"Wadda ya mean by that?" he challenged.

"Let me put it this way, Mister, uh, what is your name anyway, Sir?"

"Oaxaca Sector 27."

"I mean your first name, Sir. What is your first name?"

"Like I said, it's Oaxaca Sector 27," he said stubbornly.

"Do you not have a given name, such as John or David?" she asked curiously.

"Only a decaying Remnant would ask that dumb question. Everyone knows that the 'given name' stuff was outlawed a long time ago."

"But, for goodness' sake, why?" she asked, genuinely surprised by this news.

"Come on, come on! You *know* why! It was people like you who made ugly ethnic slurs and used hurtful name-calling when we used to have first names. But, Distrito fixed you hate mongers, didn't it?!" he spat. "We don't have first names anymore, so The People have a lot more in common now. We're happier and get along better without them."

She had been struck by that government "fix" he talked about and the dehumanizing consequences of it all. If first names were no longer given, wasn't one's individuality greatly diminished? Of course, she reasoned, surnames were still being used, so that did unify the people somewhat.

"Would you tell me, then, about your family name?" she asked.

"What do you mean, 'family name'?"

"You identified yourself as 'Oaxaca,' didn't you?" she explained.

"'Oaxaca Sector 27'," he corrected her, "but that's not a family name. They were outlawed, too. Old Remnant!" he added spitefully.

"But, do you know your family name, or your personal bloodline?" she persevered.

"What *are* you talking about, Doctor? I told you I'm Oaxaca Sector 27! That's who I am."

"So, 'Oaxaca of Sector 27' is your name and your only name, is that right?" she asked pointedly.

"Jeez! How many times do I have to tell you?" he asked, clearly exasperated. "Are you just too old and feeble to get what I'm saying?"

"No, Oaxaca Sector 27, I now understand that that is your one and only name. However, would you allow this stubborn Remnant just a few more questions?"

"Yeah," he answered, scowling.

"Is Sector 27 where you reside?" she inquired.

"If you're talking about where I live, yeah, I live in Oaxaca Sector 27."

~~~

...she was still only six and...hadn't reached the "age of reason" yet.

XII
STONE PARK

It was one of those evenings. All four children were gathered contentedly in the kitchen, basking in the heat radiating from the ancient cast iron stove. Tonight was one of those nights when Aly's daddy would come in really late, smelling stinky like the saloon in Grandpa's hotel. He would talk funny, kinda like his mouth was full of food.

As expected, Kurt Brons entered the room with twinkling eyes, robustly announcing his arrival with, "Where's Daddy's girl?" Aly ran gleefully into his arms for that powerful bear hug and a snappy chorus of "Mares eat oats 'n' does eat oats, 'n' lil' lambs eat ivy…" She was being held in his arms now, giggling happily, giving him the customary peck on his roughly stubbled cheek. Once she managed past that icky stale beer smell, it was so nummy to breathe in that familiar aroma of Old Spice. She was beaming happily when her father placed her gingerly back onto the floor. But, his face was now clouding over. Aly's innocent young brow attempted to furrow, dismayed to see something had angered him. She knew it couldn't be anything she had done, 'cause, after all,

61

she was still only six and, as he had many times explained to her and her brothers, she hadn't reached the "age of reason" yet. She followed her daddy's every movement, observing that his ritual tonight was looking pretty much the same. Kurt Brons walked over to her beautiful eldest brother, Patrick. He then squared himself in front of the boy, and shouted the same accusation he always did when he came home late like this: "And you, you lazy bum, why aren't your brothers and sister ready for bed?" The young teen's face fell and his lips began to quiver. Holding a firm stance with lips taut, the boy glared defiantly into his father's eyes. In a barely audible monotone, he gave his usual explanation; that they had been waiting for him to bring home groceries, so they could have supper first. Aly watched as her Daddy made his sudden lurch at Patrick, grab the front of the boy's dingy plaid shirt, and shove him into that awful, dark, cold room. As the children knew he would, he slammed the door angrily behind them, leaving Aly, Peter, and Paulie in the kitchen to wait things out.

The three children stood motionless, anticipating the worst. They were too frightened to look at one another, each feeling a personalized shame for being powerless to help Patrick. They huddled together in the warmth of the nearby stove, reassured by the crackling sounds of burning wood.

Then it began. First, the muffled shouts of their father, followed by a jarring "W-H-A-C-K!" The small window above the kitchen sink shuttered after the jolting thud in the next room. Aly peeked quickly at her two brothers and caught them wincing. Patrick still had not cried out.

Confusion and a deeply menacing fear gripped her young heart. "This isn't real," she assured herself firmly. "I'll just pretend it's not happening." Just as she began squeezing her eyes shut ever so tightly, Peter grabbed her hand firmly. He led his young charge to her small cot in the adjoining alcove. Having swiftly slipped beneath the security of her thin woolen blanket, he said, "Night, Al'," and tiptoed away.

"Night, Peetie," she whispered back softly and hurried to the safety of her long ago place.

"The clock was striking twelve o'clock, it smiled on us below..."

~~~

"This word, 'parents,' what does it mean?"

XIII
PEOPLE'S HALL, 13:15

"Thirteen months later, my mother produced the first of four live-birth children" Because humanoid bio-modification was then at its infancy, all four offspring - my three brothers and I - assumed only the genetic legacies of our parents; no frills and no eradication of undesirable traits, so to speak. Anyway, such genetic legacies, coupled with the effects of deeply engrained cultural norms, such as the freedom of individual choice, usually produced citizens who were inherently more independent and self-reliant than their parents before them."

"This word, 'parents,' what does it mean?" inquired an unfamiliar voice.

"Well," she answered, "simply stated, 'parents' could be considered to have the same meaning as today's 'progenitors' and, until recent decades, 'parents' was the qualifying term used specifically for the humanoid partnership of two Homo sapiens of the opposite sex. *("Am I mistaken," she thought, or did I just hear titters from the audience?")* In my youth," she continued, "and even through my early adult years, a female and male were considered requisite to the conception, production, and tutelage of their own offspring. Once the male and female produced a child, their societal status was elevated to 'parents', and their parenting responsibilities were correspondingly heightened. The most prominent differences between this designation and those utilized today are (a) parents were always human, (b) the offspring were gestated within the human female's own biological uterus, and (c) the female human gave live birth by means of her own physical body."

She heard no titters now; only the clamor of distaste. The Doctor was shaken by the palpable restlessness from her audience. Because her statements had obviously captured their attention, no one noticed the BC module's increased pulsations.

~~~

"It, it is worthy of your note that, once the non-bio-modified children survived the live birth process of separating from the biological mother's body, they became wards of their parents, not of el Distrito. By virtue of being parents, the man and woman were automatically duty- and legally bound to raise and educate their children, according to the then-societal norms. The offsprings' initial education by the parents was a prerequisite to public, government-mandated instruction. This pre-school instruction covered such matters as personal hygiene, good manners, honesty, civility, and..."

"Doctor! Permission to speak?" The Doctor peered through the blinding overhead lights, hoping to see who was calling out. As she strained to focus, the only image she was able to make out was a slowly waving, elegantly shaped, hand. Instantly recognizing its unusually configured design, she recalled that it had been created solely for those of exceedingly exceptional intellect; the protected people of Quadrant Promise. The Doctor felt a wave of profound awe as she watched the man rise and face her. Seeing him quite clearly now, she thought of the unconscionably crude results of earlier biogenetic engineering. Never had she imagined she'd live to witness such a superbly fine product as he!

"Would you please stand and identify yourself, Sir, so I may address you properly?" she asked.

"I am called Ching," he announced proudly.

"Thank you, Ching. What may I do for you, Sir?"

"Do I have your permission to speak frankly, Doctor?" he asked.

"Certainly, Ching. Please do."

"Very well. I then ask you why it is, Doctor, that you lecture on such an outmoded, as well as disagreeable, subject as humanoid history? Surely the good doctor understands that such speech was purged long ago."

"Fair question, Mr. Ching," she answered enthusiastically. "Although purged from public discourse, my core theme of self-reliance remains, I hope, a thought-provoking topic. Although it has been deemed a disagreeable subject, el Distrito did, nonetheless, authorize its discussion for today's academic exercise."

"May I inquire, esteemed Doctor, as to the purpose of your obvious attempts to provoke The People?" he insisted.

She felt titillated. *"Could it be that this compelling fellow is actually someone who exercises independent thought?"* She tilted her head coyly toward her handsome challenger, thirsty to engage him. "Well, Sir, it is my belief that intellectual change is best promoted through stimulated discussion, and that stimulation is often the direct result of unorthodox – and even heretofore purged – speech. Of course, as Distrito citizens, we are all very much aware that any attempt to execute cultural exchange is unquestionably illegal; certainly would never be exercised by a mere Remnant, such as myself. Furthermore, my talk is not made in an attempt to promote such change. Rather, today's presentation is no more than an exercise in facetiousness, mere entertainment, as I suggested to the audience earlier."

After what seemed an eternity of deafening silence, he said, "Amusing, Dear Doctor, most amusing."

~~~

Having met the morning's toughness challenge, she ... smirked defiantly into her brother's laughing eyes.

XIV
KEEPING UP

Holding the Budweiser bottles at arms' length, Peter, Aly, and Patrick trudged along the muddy path leading to the alley out back. "Why doesn't Paulie ever have to empty these things?" ten-year-old Peter complained. Although he was being really careful, some of the day's excretions sloshed out of a bottle, over the rim, and onto his hands. Aly didn't notice him grimace in disgust. She knew to keep walking and concentrate on the rutted trail beneath her.

"Because Paulie's with Dad today, that's why," Patrick snapped. "Now, let's hurry up, you two! There're more in the house and Dad'll be home soon." At that, they both followed their older brother's lead in silence, hurrying to empty the amber-colored bottles in their charge. The three then jogged back to the house for the next load.

Aly was in full trot to keep up with her brothers, as the threesome repeated again and again their back-and-forth trip to the stinky alley. She thought how lucky the boys were to be able to use her

71

daddy's beer bottles to pee in. Whether they were in the house or the car, they simply handed the bottles to each other whenever they felt the need. Aly thought how unfair it was that, when she had to go, she had to wait for her daddy to lift her to the utility sink, if they were home, or, if her daddy was driving, stop the car and find her a well hidden place off the side of the road. Those roadside occasions really were unfair, especially when it was snowing. Even though her father would lead her by the hand to the seclusion of nearby bushes or large tree trunk, then turn and step away for the sake of her modesty, she never felt like she really had privacy. The boys would be stifling their giggles when their father and she returned to the car. "Why can't I use the bottles like the boys, Daddy?" she pouted.

"That's just the difference between girls and boys, Al'," he'd say. Although his answer wasn't much comfort, the obedient six-year-old kept quiet. Once Daddy explained something, that was that! After all, he did know best about everything, she reflected in adoration. Anyhow, the fact that her beloved brothers even allowed her to join in and help them with this daily cleanup chore and she wasn't even seven yet – somehow made up for her exclusion from the uniquely masculine activity of bottle peeing.

The urine-soaked alley was, at times, also a place of adventure for Aly and her brother. They loved racing there from school, especially after heavy rainstorms. Peetie could quickly locate the crawdads in the yucky pools of dark water. "Aw, Aly, pick 'em up, like…this!" he'd shout, swiftly plucking three mud-green crayfish from their murky home. He was always proud to display his fearlessness to his admiring sidekick. After one fluid swoop, he would hold up the protesting captives directly under Aly's impish Gaelic nose. It tickled Peter when he could get his little sister to shrink with horror at the wriggling antennae and jerking jointed legs. But today Aly stubbornly refused to give him the satisfaction Of "being a baby." Having met the morning's toughness challenge, she placed her feet solidly beneath her, smirking defiantly into her brother's laughing eyes. Knowing she had passed another one of his "sissy" tests, her innocent heart rejoiced. Life was complete, knowing Peetie was still proud of her.

~~~

"Doctor," the man spoke softly, *"do you wish to partake with the others?"*

XV
PEOPLE'S HALL, 13:46

His eyes held fast upon hers. Beyond the amusement, she saw understanding, coupled with...could it be...respect? She looked back to the audience, hoping to get a quick take on their reaction to Ching's comments. Nothing. Although directed toward the podium, their eyes appeared vacant, disengaged, seeing nothing.

"Further to early 21st Century parenting," she continued, "the home was the very foundation of any offspring's overall edification. It wasn't until 2027 that The People ceded total authority over such activities to el Distrito and..." A piercingly high-pitched alert screeched through the air, its suddenness enough to jolt the heart into spasm. The Doctor watched inquiringly as the entire audience rose in regimented cadence and undulated its way along the outside aisles. They shuffled in unison toward the yawn of two awaiting portals.

A soothing, melodic voice was speaking: "Ciudadanos! Please move to the nearest exit to enjoy your mid-morning reward. El Distrito has generously granted us the customary twenty minutes to enjoy our preferred gratification. Please, let us all indulge ourselves fully before returning to today's lecture, but not before giving thanks to Distrito. We all know we are provided this morning's gift because...because, why?" the voice prompted.

"Because we deserve it!" they shouted enthusiastically. "Yes, we deserve it!" they chanted again. "El Distrito provides because we deserve it!" The Doctor remained motionless, fascinated by the ritualized exodus. Once the last attendee had filed out of the room, she felt oddly comforted, knowing that she was now alone with her new friend from Quadrant Tigres.

"Doctor," the man spoke softly, "do you wish to partake with the others?"

"I do not, Sir!" she snapped. Had she looked at that instant, she would have seen the playful grin on his handsomely configured face.

Not wanting to show her embarrassment, she turned from him and began reviewing her lectern notes. Minutes passed and not a sound. The silence became unbearable. The Doctor daringly raised her head ever so slowly until her line of vision revealed Ching seated leisurely in a nearby on-stage chair. His long legs were crossed in complete composure and his captivating six-digit hands were clasped haughtily behind his beautifully toned neck. She no longer avoided those exquisite sapphire eyes! He smiled boldly, laughingly. Guardedly, she smiled back.

~~~

...she liked the way they seemed to respect him,

XVI
JUST ONE OF THE BOYS, 1951 AD

Peter looked back over his shoulder and saw Aly dutifully keeping up, stepping carefully into his shoe tracks. "Wanna go to the tree, Aly?"

"Sure!" she said cheerfully. As they walked in tandem toward the Friedens' place, Peter squatted now and then to grab an unsuspecting creature slithering across the path. "I'll get yours, too, Al', OK?" Without waiting for his sister's answer, he plucked up three smaller specimens, which, seemingly without a care, undulated contentedly about his forearms.

As they drew closer, her nostrils bristled from the groping stench of the old Red Cedar. Aly wanted him to hurry up and get it over with, so they could go home. But, she knew she'd have to be patient, until he had completed the self-glorifying ritual. She saw the Frieden boys on the knoll, just ahead. They were waving frantically for her and Peter to hurry over.

These 9- and 10-year-old boys were obvious scrappers. Aly had never seen so many scabs and fresh cuts, and she had three pretty tough brothers. She looked at them in wonder to realize they were really big boys, almost as big as Patrick and Paulie, who were lots older. Although much taller and heavier than Peetie, she liked the way they seemed to respect him, like he was the boss.

"Hey, Pete, how many did ya bring?" asked Eddie, the bigger Frieden boy, reaching for her brother's bounty. Peter grinned mischievously, as he lifted the writhing green garters high over his head. Then, in an exaggerated display of might, he tossed all three of them at his filthy friend, who giggled approvingly. The captives flopped onto the ground and lay there, as though dazed from the impact of their fall. Eddie scrambled to gather them up then quickly spun around and raced his brother gleefully to the old beleaguered tree.

Eddie and his brother couldn't hurl the now-limp garters thrown onto the overhead branches fast enough. The once-proud Cedar awaited, already laden with rotting fragments of earlier offerings. The dogs were frenzied, braying at their soon-to-be trophies.

It was horrifying! Aly could not believe that the innocent game of scooping up these graceful creatures could turn into the nightmare she now felt compelled to witness. The husky mutt with a lobbed-off ear and sprinkling of spots seized a mid-sized snake with a fearsome snarl. "Poor, poor baby snake," she thought. "It didn't want to be taken away from its mommy," she commiserated. She had no choice but to tough it out and watch the carnage. She had to prove to Peetie that she could take it, just like any boy. She prayed silently that the tears welling in her eyes would not give her away.

The second dog, a young terrier mix, happily following suit, bounded excitedly upward, snapping at its selected prey. The beautifully colored garter snakes were twitching erratically now, seemingly agitated to know their awaiting fate. A primal surge shot through their smooth, sleek bodies, catapulting them toward the higher branches, but to no avail; no sooner did the writhing reptiles stretch desperately skyward, that they lost their grips on their last chance for survival. Aly shuttered as they each fell helplessly into the impatiently snapping jaws below.

Hearing sounds of ripping flesh and the victorious howls of Peter and his friends, Aly could bear no more. "I'll just go away," she reassured herself. She squeezed her eyes tightly shut and the afternoon's nightmare began to ebb. As it was being replaced by a soothing, comforting song, the small child began to smile.

"With folded hands it seemed to say, we'll miss you if you go...

And we just couldn't say goodbye"

~~~

...her deepest instinct told her she was his prey.

XVII
PEOPLE'S HALL, 14:02

The satiation period was over and the crowd was returning. Had the attendees bothered to look to the dais, they would have seen that the woman and her challenger had not moved since the break began twenty minutes earlier. The two were still standing, nearly toe-to-toe, as though frozen in the moment. The mirth showed on Ching's proud masculine mouth, as he playfully held the Doctor's searching gaze. Their eyes shared a profound familiarity that she couldn't yet decipher. "Before I resume my talk," she said conspiratorially, her lips barely moving, "please tell me, whoever you are, Sir, whether your intention is to mock or simply provoke me to my own undoing."

"Elegant Lady, all I will say is that I am a lifelong devotee of your work. I simply could not resist coming today."

Could she trust him? Her extensive experience with Just Conduct Oversight had been devastating. Enough so that she'd rather receive a physical thrashing than again be subjected to its enforcement. Its imprint left her trusting no one, especially anyone younger than she, who could not possibly relate to her objective view of recent Distrito history. But, there was something oddly compelling about this man. Those sensational Tigres eyes spoke of sincere interest in her and what she had to say. At the same time, though, she was disturbed by the calculated precision of his every move. The sight of him triggered the image of a crouching feline, waiting patiently for its optimum moment to pounce. No, there was no doubt; her deepest instinct told her she was his prey.

"Your fictional accounts of humanoid culture I find particularly entertaining," he said quietly. She was startled by his choice of words; to call her words "fictional" was jarring. If he sincerely believed she was promulgating untruths, she was in danger. Although his charm had begun to delude her, this was clearly her wakeup call; i.e., he just might be officially monitoring her speech today. *"I must be more careful,"* she chastised herself silently.

"I'm so pleased you find my lecture entertaining," she whispered sarcastically. "Now, if you'll be so kind as to take your seat, I'll attempt to amuse the others as well." With twinkling eyes, Ching sighed wistfully. Giving a deep theatrical bow, he turned, and took his leave. As he stepped off the stage, her eyes followed him, very much annoyed at the pleasure she was feeling to watch his powerful stride.

The Doctor changed her attention to the returning audience. She marveled at the new order of things; the most dark-skinned females enjoyed a more favored social status over those of lighter skins, so they reclaimed their seats first. She expected the males would be re-entering the hall, the darker ones first and the lighter following, but only after every single female had returned to their seats. This practice was one of the more benign diktats of Distrito social justice. Allowing one to walk in front was no longer a voluntary display of courtesy, but a legislated display of subservience. Strange, she mused, how the prior century's political movement to achieve "same work, same pay" had manifested itself into the stipulated degradation of today's males. Even stranger, she thought, that a preferential societal status was now determined by skin tone; the darker, the more esteemed. *"Thank God Dr. King cannot see us now!"* she thought ruefully.

While attendees continued the return to their assigned chairs, the Doctor noticed a young female standing defiantly by the southeast entrance. She had large black eyes, dark skin, and unusually short stature; all suggesting a strong Aztec-Mayan ancestry. She certainly typified the highly revered Distrito woman, the Doctor thought. *"If I recall correctly,"* she thought to herself, *"it was back in 2022 when such ethnic physiology was adopted as the more desirable traits of The People's gene pool. "*

"Young woman, do you have something to say?" Startled, the female looked up. Her moist dark eyes darted angrily about the room before fixing on the speaker. With motionless lips, a simulation of her angry, trembling voice rang out.

~~~

...she, too, would from this day forward be held responsible for whatever she did and did not do.

XVIII
THE AGE OF REASON

Aly had reached her 7th birthday, a point in time when she would begin to be taken seriously and held accountable for any transgressions. This was an honoured benchmark she could now share with her beloved brothers. How exciting! Her brothers could really be proud of her and think of her as one of them. Just as they have been, she, too, would from this day forward be held responsible for whatever she did and did not do. With her 6th year behind her, her daddy must judge her in a grownup way from now on, and evaluate her actions seriously. No more would she be looked upon as a little kid who did not know how to live up to and respect the rules. Best of all, she would not have to endure that accusatory chant of "She's just a child that doesn't know any better; after all, she hasn't reached the age of reason yet," one time more! "The boys can be proud of me, 'cause Daddy will show them I have to 'take it like a Mensch' now, too," she thought dreamily.

She was reliving the evening of that birthday when her father had asked, "Aly Girl, did you see what the boys and I got you?" She looked in the direction he was pointing and saw a shoe box wrapped in semi-glossy butcher's paper and scratchy tan twine. It had been perfectly centered on the kitchen table beside a small unfrosted cake sporting seven red lighted candles. The tiny flames were flickering in happy unison. "Wow!" she thought, keeping her distance from the package. She wanted to move closer to get a better whiff of the tempting treat, but was unsure of whether it would be OK. The 7-year-old birthday girl looked over to her father for a sign of what to do next.

"Go ahead, Kiddo. It's for you," he responded lovingly. Having her daddy's approval, Aly stepped up to the table, her little heart racing with anticipation. "Blow out the candles, Aly!" he and her three brothers prompted excitedly. Being duly encouraged, she quickly bent over the inviting Bundt cake.

"Don't forget to make a wish," the boys chimed, as their little sister quickly squeezed her eyes shut, hesitated the perfunctory split second, then blew out all the dancing flames in one exuberant gust. While the room echoed four pairs of loudly clapping hands, she looked up to see adoring faces, smiling widely with warm affection.

Her father then nodded toward the awaiting package. "Aren't you going to open your birthday present, Aly?"

~~~

*"We're' all processed in the exact same way.
Production codes make sure of this."*

XIX
PEOPLES HALL, 14:16

"First, I'm not a 'young woman,' so don't disrespect me. I have a name, you know; it's Salinas Sector 2. Second, this fairytale story of yours, I used to hear rumors about it a long time ago. Why do you come here today? Just to tell those lies again? Even the way you talk about your people and what you remember about it is prohibido. And that junk about kids being raised by male and female parents! Do you think we're so stupid we'd believe that sexist basura? You know el Distrito will always protect us from your lies. So, are you here just to get attention? If it is, Remnant, just understand this: We pay no attention to your worn out stories, because we know what they really are; big fat lies. We have to stay here today until you're finished with your speech, OK? But, just stop feeding us all this garbage, all right? No matter what you say, we know that all Sector People are equal in every way. We're all processed in the exact same way. Production codes make sure of this. So, get real, Doctor! And, just so you know: At the end of the day, we're gonna grade your lying lecture. We're gonna tell it like it is; especially the parts about males and females birthing and schooling their products. Lies! Sin vergüenza, disgusting lies!

"Young woman," she began...

"Stop calling me that, you stupida!" the female voice sputtered.

"I figure your brain doesn't work right, 'cause you're so old, but, it's still not right for you to diss us like this!"

The Doctor winced at her adversary's caustic remarks. She knew the female's accusation was, in part, true; she had been making illegal references, using terminology that had been outlawed years ago. *"Yes, of course, it was back in 2022," she recalled to herself silently, "'The Year of Coalescence.' Since that transnational ban, unfathomable amounts of 'illicit' documents and data had been confiscated and warehoused for the People's protection. Today, after more than thirty years, that information probably still awaits bureaucratic scrutiny prior to sanctioned public access. Once propriety is established, systematic redaction is undertaken prior to actual release to the People. Be that as it may, whether this young woman is a plant or not, I simply cannot allow her to waste more of my time. I've got to get through to someone! Anyone!"*

"I do apologize to you...to everyone, Citizen, and assure you that my reference to genders was merely an attempt to encourage academic exercise. It was never intended to offend." Her eyes looked beyond the Aztec beauty and were met with an entire auditorium of frosty stares. "It certainly is not my intention to offend you," she persisted. "I realize that the objective exercises I set up for today are unknown to you, but if you'll allow me to continue, I will do my best to answer your earlier question in more acceptable terms. In brief, I beg your indulgence until I have finished presenting. Only when I have completed the core points of my talk will you have the necessary conceptual data needed to evaluate what I've come here to say. "

The old woman felt drained. The day had been long and intense. Her lower back and conspicuously shapely calves ached horribly from so many hours of standing. Although a brief oxygenation break could be arranged, taking time from this last-ditch effort was simply out of the question. If she were to have any real chance of actually getting through to someone out there, she could not allow herself to falter now. She didn't need to refer to the Deviance Permit inside her jacket pocket to know she would never be given another chance after today. She quietly considered how to best continue without creating more distractions. The young woman remained standing, seemingly appeased. She was still angry, though, as evidenced by silky dark brows tightly knitted over squinting Latin eyes and hefty brown arms crossed defiantly over her chest.

Pushing forward, the Doctor discreetly cleared her dry throat. "I'm so glad you mentioned separate genders. When I was of collegiate age, there were three scientifically accepted biological sexes. 'Gender' has since come to replace the word 'sex' in Distrito-condoned vernacular. Now, before you get too upset with my choice of words," she said hurriedly, "please remember that today's lecture has been specifically authorized to provoke you. El Distrito has authorized this provocation for the purpose of evaluating your responses to this blatantly unorthodox presentation by me, a mere Remnant. After my presentation today, each of you will be required to participate in an official evaluation of today's presentation. In that questionnaire, you will be asked to discuss your reactions, if any, to the unusual terminology I have been using. Ultimately, you will be asked to judge whether my speech has been so preposterous that it can only be deemed as meaningless rhetoric, with no basis in reality whatsoever. You will also be asked to reveal whether you would not deem it so. So, you see," she breathed in deeply to calm herself, "since your evaluation is officially required, you and I are in this together, so to speak, at least for the remainder of my Permitted speaking time. You'll be relieved to know, however, that our time here today has a precise expiration, and that expiration draws near. That said, and with your collective permission, I will do my best to forge through my talking points, so that you'll be equipped with all the information you need to complete your questionnaires. In return for that permission, I will do my utmost not to aggravate the more sensitive among you." She looked over to the dark young woman, who now appeared to be somewhat less confrontational.

"Excellent! It looks as though we're all in agreement, so I'll move on," she confirmed. "As I was saying, please understand that 'gender' and 'sex' are two terms that have pronounced societal implications which I ask you to consider. Remember, please, the parameters I now set before you are requisite to today's academic exercise."

~~~

"Life is not meant to be easy, Aly."

XX
GROWING UP

It was magical being young, single, and self-reliant! Aly loved the exhilaration she felt coursing through her body. It drove her to live her life with purpose. She hungered to investigate all things new to her that were not frivolous. Her innate understanding that life on this earthly plane was all too brief and finite caused in her a sense of constant urgency. It propelled her to painstakingly pursue those studies that promised to satisfy her ever-present curiosity. Although she loved spending time at the nearby library to research varied subjects of interest, Aly determined they'd have to take a back seat to learning those concepts and skills that would improve her chances for success. She was a vibrant 23-year-old, who utterly hated not knowing the true longevity of the Australian platypus, or understanding its ultimate purpose within the Animal Kingdom, and how she, as a lone individual, could adequately construct a livable home from foundation to roof. It grated on her nerves that each and every day was too short to accommodate all she yearned to study and do, which was just about anything and everything required to make her self-sufficient.

It exasperated her that there were just too few hours in the day. Between maintaining her own apartment and vehicle, working from morning to evening at the electronics firm, then attending auto mechanics at Santa Monica Community College vehicle depot in the late evenings, she found it hard as heck to keep her eyes open long enough to finish the reading she had assigned for the day before dropping off to sleep. As it was, Aly was now rising in the dark of morning to practice Spanish verb conjugations before heading for the office. It was necessary to fill every hour constructively, though, if she were to accomplish anything of consequence or value. This she understood as her own personal commandment.

Aly admitted her impatience for those peers whom she judged to be either silly, juvenile, or without specific, self-defined direction. The ones who acted irresponsibly or without honour she refused to engage. After all, life on this plane was a short-lived opportunity and there was so much to experience! There was just too much to do to allow the distraction of those who did not share, or could not understand life's urgency. Besides, she didn't want to be associated with such stupidity.

With pungent revere, Aly recalled Mr. Trice, her Spartan and profoundly dedicated Aikido instructor. He had demonstrated to her the unavoidably painful path to accomplishment through unwavering self-discipline, as well as the rewards of dignity and pure humility. She remained grateful to this proud retired Marine for pointing out the undignified childishness of most Americanized dojos, especially those of trendy liberalized teachings. It still irked her to think of those artificial rankings of pink, purple, and orange belts. It cheapened the integrity of traditional martial arts!

With vivid clarity, she remembered the National Black Belt exhibition he had invited her and several brown belts to attend. It took them a twenty-minute drive to reach the august Westchester stadium. She could still feel her shock at watching the ruthlessly sadistic exhibition match between Judo and Karate black belts. The vulgar blood-thirsty clamor from the stands was totally unexpected; where was the serenely proud execution of each movement? How startled she was by the sound of a fracturing forearm. She'd never heard that soft cracking noise before, so it took her brain a second or two to deduce what she was hearing. It was just too surreal to make sense of. Somehow it was no surprise when Mr. Trice abruptly insisted they leave.

He looked deeply saddened, as he drove them back to get their cars in silence. Once back at the dojo, the others jumped out. "Thanks for the great time, Mr. Trice," they chimed. Aly watched them running excitedly to their cars, hearing one of them shout, "Man! Did ya get a load of how that one guy got totally aced?! 'Bet they had to call for an ambulance! Was that great, or what?!"

"Aly, I owe you an apology," Mr. Trice was saying. "It wanted you to see the true dignity of Aikido today, a ceremony of precise control, performed with humility and honour. Instead you saw

the shameless antics of stupid jerks. Completely undisciplined! Their street fighting antics were disgusting!"

"But, weren't the Black Belt skills we saw today what we all work for?" she asked, perplexed.

"Ah! You'd think so, wouldn't you." He peered onto the car hood before him, the overhead street lights reflecting off his tired eyes. "But, you're aware of how crude those so-called Black Belts were, aren't you?"

"Yes," she admitted calmly, beginning to understand the depth of his displeasure.

"Do you think those fools even came close to understanding the dignity of the masters?" Without waiting for her answer, he added, "Do you believe those immature fools had the right to the revered status of regional exhibition? Don't you see how insulting it is to the very integrity of martial arts to allow those idiots to perform at such an event? Why, they showed no dignity!" he spat. "No dignity at all! They should be 86'd from any dojo that devoutly follows the masters. Aly," he added pleadingly, "can't you see the insult of it all? I mean, they spat in the faces of all of us who work so hard to uphold our fidelity to an art of perfectly synced mental and physical discipline. Those snot nosed kids back there wanted only to show what big, bad men they are, but they showed me only that they are undisciplined street fighters, using deadly tools they have no right to. No," he shook his bowed head slowly, "they have no idea what humility means."

"Yes, Sir, it truly is an insult," she whispered. And she also understood how irresponsible those martial arts studios were that produced those Black Belts who fought today. Yes, "fought" would be the right word. Instead of humbly exhibiting their mastery of the arts, they chose to dishonour them with their hoodlum-like nonsense. Those students were obviously the products of commercialized dojos that mislead students with the gratification of premature rankings; achievements that really were never earned. Those silly brightly colored belts, premature badges of accomplishment, were misleading and dangerously wrong. Aly was personally aware of some nearby dojos that would hand out such belts to students who had trained for only a matter of months! Those children would often feel cocky after being wrongly honoured with distinction by their trainers and peers. Many never went on to complete any serious training or earn any credible ranking. Such was the result of the "feel good" American culture; no one is better than any one else, no child should feel the bite of disappointing failure, no effort was unappreciated, everyone was a winner. What deception!

Mr. Trice made no secret of his own hard-earned martial arts accomplishments. Whenever his students began complaining that the mat work was difficult, or whined about the throbbing pains of being slammed to the mat, Master Trice would tell his story: As a Marine Corps. Corporal, Mr. Trice was stationed in Seoul. During that time, he spent every liberty studying under a twelfth degree-belt master. After four intense years of arduous ascetic training and, what seemed like an unending flood of setbacks, he was rewarded.

His revered master wordlessly bestowed upon him, still a striving Brown Belt, in a most austere ceremony, the master's recognition of his excellence as a first-degree Aikido Black Belt. That astonishing life lesson of deserving, well-earned merit was from that point forward infused in him as his defining moral imperative. Today, that hard work, and sustained self-discipline had brought him to third degree Black Belt status and his strict adherence to traditional martial arts methods had become the essence of his own teaching.

"Life is not meant to be easy, Aly. We're cheating all our kids to have them believe otherwise."

~~~

"...self-reliance is of little value or consequence in today's world..."

XXI
PEOPLE'S HALL, 14:21

"Second only to their gifts of procreation, male and female parents ingrained within their offspring the critical concepts and skills needed for healthy societal interaction. They generally accomplished this in the privacy of their own home where they taught each child, by example, the dignity of one's individual merit and how that merit is the reward of living up to one's personal and civic responsibilities in a self-reliant way. That training was usually incorporated within the family's routine activities. By observing their parents' day-to-day behavior, out of respect for their parental authority, the children quite naturally grew to respect that behavior, mimic it, and eventually exemplify it throughout adulthood. This teaching method was a truly constructive..."

"Doctor!" he interrupted, "why you bring up such archaic practices as humanoid procreation and child rearing, I simply cannot venture to guess. Did not our Council of Enhancement decree long ago that formative training by biological parents was contraindicative to The People's more enlightened pursuits?"

Ching's voice simulations were reverberating shrilly, urging her to get to the point. "After all," he continued, "it is well known that the two-sex gender distinction was found by your Supreme Court Justices to be clearly repressive and discriminatory and, therefore, destructive to an orderly society. You and I know full well, Dear Doctor, that the roles of 'father' and 'mother' were pragmatically abolished long ago, and for very good reason. Today, our society enjoys an ever-expanding gender tolerance, one which perpetually provides the joys of unlimited variety and preference flexibility."

They simultaneously glanced up to assess the students' reaction to his confrontational remarks. Neither saw any students whosoever. The Hall was completely empty. Then noticing a flashing module over each exit, they surmised that the audience had been called to Rewards and, in the intensity of their exchange, they hadn't even noticed. Returning their eyes to each other, they nodded slowly, tacitly agreeing to continue without the others. The Doctor felt a vague sense of pleasure in having Ching to herself for the next few moments. That pleasure was disturbingly familiar, and yet she couldn't recall anything specific. She shook it off as a distracting nuance, reminding herself to stay focused. Time was running out.

"Yes, Mr. Ching," she sighed heavily, "you've described the very calamity I'm trying to address. The direct rearing by then-traditional female mothers and male fathers had a profoundly wholesome effect on our children, the benefits of which enriched society in countless ways. For instance, dignified adult behavior was the intentional aim of their hands-on child rearing, and that dignity was generated by a disciplined respect for rules of courtesy and duty. Male fathers stressed duty to family, respectful regard for elders, and an overriding reverence for mothers as keepers of the hearth...so to speak. Female mothers personified the very dignity of motherhood; the essence of which instilled the knowledge of safety, nurturing, and compassion for the innocent within the child. The respectful conduct of a well-reared child was considered to be the most essential component to civilized interaction with others."

"Dignity of parenting! Such whimsical nonsense, Doctor!" he chided, now grinning. "You and I know full well that dignity is a ridiculous patrician concept and its pretentious practices resulted in painful and damaging disregard for far too many. Surely you remember those pompous elitists who strode about proclaiming that dignified behavior was the hallmark of civility! And," he prodded, "you must also remember how oppressive that standard was to those who preferred to assert themselves in more expressive ways! You do recall, don't you, Doctor, when that thoughtless discrimination necessitated The Council's very formation!"

He was growing more impatient. How she wanted to lash back at him. But, she wasn't convinced that he really believed what he was saying, or that he enjoyed backing her into a dangerously incriminating corner this way. The old woman was aware of a gnawing fatigue, but didn't dare give in to it. She had to keep any semblance of her weakness and growing sense of futility under wraps until she had finished what she had come to the Hall to do. Time was running out and Ching was intentionally sidetracking her from that goal.

The Doctor remembered quite well that period to which Ching referred. It was when angry mobs ruled by intimidation, as well as undertaking disgustingly crude and barbaric acts; the pathetically senseless violence of petulant children. Her heart ached thinking back to the mindless brutality they had wreaked; how they had physically injured innocent people for no reason other than they were in their way; how their vulgarity and inhumanity knew no limits as they attacked others. "Yes, Mr. Ching, I can still recall those horrors. They were the unpardonable crimes of undisciplined mobs revolting against individuals who had earned more wealth and acquired a more comfortable lifestyle than they. Individuals who respected the rule of law. Individuals whom they did not know, personally or otherwise. The violence they perpetrated was unconscionable. It was a painfully shameful time for our people," she added pensively.

"Then you agree, don't you, Doctor, that the Council's first official action – out of real need – simply had to be to protect The People from future outbreaks of their own understandable anger; the Council had to ensure equality for *all* The People, rather than a select few. That could only be done by preventing abhorrent patrician conduct from dividing The People. Now that those elitist practices have been systemically rooted out, today's codified law demands our complete and open acceptance of *all* genders, as well as each and every one of their sexual practices, which has taken its rightful place within our culture.

"Of course, all that silliness occurred long before the production of most of today's attendees, so they are spared any understanding of such crippling discrimination. Yes, dear Doctor, one can only wonder at how very much improved our society has become as a result of the Council's cultural correction," he smiled. "Just think of it! The People are no longer bound by those misguided and hurtful cultural distinctions. They are now comfortably protected, completely enveloped by Distrito care."

Being alone with him was no longer pleasant. *"Where in the devil is the audience? This is the very conversation they need to be exposed to!"* she thought. "But, Sir," she persisted, "is it not self evident that without honourable conduct, which demands adult restraint, neither man-nor womankind can ever hope to enjoy the empowerment of self-reliance?"

"Oh, stop it!" he snapped. "Just take a look around and you will see a People who enjoy a cultural climate of never-before-imagined ease. There is nothing they want for. Do you expect them to disavow their secure, self-indulgent lives in exchange for your twisted concept of self-reliance? Listen, Madam, self-reliance generally requires independent thinking, a strong work ethic to reach one's targeted purpose, and self-imposed restraint from opposing distractions. Surely we can agree that individual self-reliance is of little consequence in today's world, can't we, Doctor?"

Ching was becoming increasingly confrontational. In light of this, his earlier hints of camaraderie were puzzling. However, the fact that he just addressed her as "Madam" was indicative of decorum not seen in public life for several generations. "Well, perhaps I'm just imagining things – placing too much emphasis on subtlety," she thought." But she didn't really think so. And yet, it was highly probable that he'd been sent here today to negatively assess her presentation. Yes, his growing provocations strongly pointed to it. Still, her deeply felt sense was that this polished and articulate man was not the enemy, but the very blessing she had been praying for.

"You actually believe," he continued tauntingly, "that the lives of The People are somehow lacking without this 'self-reliance' business, don't you?" She said nothing, her gaze locked onto the auditorium doors. "Very well!" he conceded, "please explain this 'dignity' of which you speak. Just how was such an ego-centric, self-elevating belief system ever condoned when its very practice openly excluded the social and economic enhancement of so many?"

"Where are those students?" she thought agitatedly.

She knew she could not – must not – return his visual contact. His compelling Tigres eyes disturbed her; they evoked stirrings of deep, dark memories cloaked in a vague, but very real, sense of alarm. Exactly what those memories were, she just couldn't put her finger on. *"Keep focused,"* she scolded herself silently.

"Won't you at least admit," Ching prompted, "that the barbaric patrician practice of gender exclusion was meant to perpetuate the ridiculous doctrine of masculine superiority?"

"No, my able opponent, I would not admit that. To the contrary! However, let's not stray from the main subject; we were discussing dignified behavior, were we not?" she added curtly.

"Of course, you're right, Doctor, except for your reference to me as your opponent," he added softly, eyes twinkling. "Nevertheless, might I first have the courtesy of your response to my question? Gender exclusion is, after all, a malignant act about which all within these walls are anxious to know your stand."

At his mention of "these walls" she warily glanced at the nearest transducer. *"I knew it! He wants me to publically admit to subversive thought!"*

~~~

...like she, it was well-maintained, attractive, and almost absent of impractical knick knacks and feminine frills.

XXII
ALL GROWN UP

She still revered him with the same adoration she had felt as a child. His nearness today made her feel safe and reassured somehow, just as it had in earlier years.

He had just called from a public phone booth at the corner deli. "I'm coming to see your new digs, My Girl," he announced with his characteristic good cheer. The phone call was his way of giving her some advance notice of his completely unexpected visit. She smiled lovingly at his feeble effort to extend her such courtesy; the corner market was only minutes away. The pressure from his impromptu visit was mounting now; there was barely enough time to check her makeup and quickly tidy things up. Fortunately, she had shopped for this week's budgeted groceries the day before, so she'd be able to offer him a decent, home-cooked lunch. Acknowledging this, the burden of being unprepared somewhat eased.

At the very instant she had finished placing two mats and silverware settings on the small dining table, Aly heard his brisk knocks at the door. With a heart brimming with gladness, she hurried to let her father in. Hastily smoothing back her sun bleached hair, she put on her sweetest smile and swung the door open with the enthusiasm he had come to expect of her.

But, how saddened she was to see how poorly he looked; his once- strong, fit frame was laden with grotesque mounds of fat, and his once sharply chiseled face was now covered with a soft flesh of disturbing deep red blotches of broken blood vessels. All this mattered not one bit, however; she would concentrate on the wonderful fact that this endearing man had made the long drive to be with her. So, with her usual determination, the heavy, aging man's image was overlooked. The only thing that really mattered was that her beloved daddy stood before her. Yes, he was beautifully fit, muscular, and just as vibrant and handsome as ever. "Hi, Dad!" she said vivaciously. "What a nice surprise!"

Sitting across from his daughter at the tiny-sized table, Aly's father looked approvingly about the small, but open room. This pleased her, for she had been fastidious about choosing an apartment she wouldn't be ashamed to have visitors in; one that was utilitarian, clean, and within her budget. It had taken several years to position herself financially to where she no longer needed a roommate to help pay the rent. She was so proud to finally be able to live alone now, be independent, and answer to no one.

Her single unit was located on the ground floor of a two-story apartment building of battered cream-colored stucco. Because it was situated at the back near the parking garage, she paid $12 a month less than a comparable unit closer to the front entrance.

As her father looked about her new home, he saw that it was modestly furnished and an austere, Spartan-like décor. In the living room area was a well-worn Naugahyde sofa that had seen its better days. It was on rollers and was neatly tucked half way under a corner table that housed a bolted-down reading lamp. It was a practical design; looking at it casually, one would never take the sofa for a pull-out bed. The doorway to its right led to the three-quarter bath and small closet alcove, where two perfectly pressed work outfits could be seen hanging neatly on metal hangers. Further to the right and adjacent to the dining area was an opening that gave full view of a miniature-like, no-frills kitchen. Although large enough to accommodate only one user at a time, he noted it had all the essentials; a waist-high white enamel refrigerator, a two-burner gas stove, small single-basin sink with utility counter on its right. His quivering mouth gave way to grinning. This whole place was a reflection of his daughter; like she, it was well-maintained, attractive, and almost absent of impractical knick knacks and feminine frills.

The afternoon sunshine streamed warmly through the miniscule open window on the back wall. Aly was thankful she had splurged at the store yesterday by purchasing the fragrant sprig of carnations poised on the sill. Although a frivolous expenditure, its yellow brilliance seemed to accent the specialness of her father's visit, while lending a touch of credibility to her new home. "You've set up a nice place for yourself, Princess," he said brightly.

Their time together wafted along pleasantly. She had served a small canned Hormel honey baked ham with aged cheddar cheese for sandwiches. Her father, not surprisingly, contributed to the occasion with several invitingly chilled cans of Coors. Aly felt such pride as she ceremoniously sliced the sharp cheddar brick into wafer-thin sheets. It was with great grandeur she demonstrated to her father that at least some of his earlier instruction had not been in vane. He had been so right about "the thinner the slice, the more flavorful the sandwich." Glancing up for his approval, she saw he was, indeed, pleased by this gesture. "Aly, the few things I've taught you, you've learned very well. That's gonna be one dee-lish sandwich!" Yes, no matter his outward appearance, this man would always be her prince, her first love. She smiled at him lovingly and he smiled back.

Kurt Brons reached clumsily for the heavy brown sack he had placed under his chair. As he pulled out another can of what had become room-temperature beer, Aly calculated that it would make his eleventh; the last of today's supply. "For all that I have tried to do for you, Little Aly," he slurred, "I know I've failed mostly. But, I think... nope... I'm convinced... I can at least teach you one really important lesson about life. Do you wanna know what that is, Aly Girl?" She nodded silently, truly anxious to hear him out. At that, he slugged down several hefty gulps of Coors. "OK!" he announced. "This is it: Always remember that my gift to you and your brothers hasn't been me as a shining example of what you SHOULD do with your lives. Nope! Instead of that, I've been your glaring example of what NOT to do." He reached over the table

116

top and took her hand. "Kind of a 'Do as I say, not as I do' kind o' thing, you know?"

How tormented this man was! Even though he had missed much of her childhood and teen years, her love for him had never wavered. Not once had she ever doubted his devotion to her and the boys. By today's standards, she had every right not to forgive him for all those missed years, the lack of basic groceries, a warm winter jacket, and that unforgettable pain of embarrassment for having to wear hand-me-downs to school. But, being upset with him had never ever occurred to her. Why, this was her daddy, after all; the man whom she had always honoured. Without a word, Aly stood up and stepped to her father's side, where she carefully sat on his lap and firmly wrapped her strong, young arms about his haggard, quaking shoulders. They clung to each other in a healing timelessness. While he sobbed, she held him firmly, her mournful green eyes welling with tears.

His Ford Taurus had purred out of the narrow driveway onto the main boulevard that would lead him home. How good their visit had been! She felt so glad to have been able to offer her father a decent meal. At the same time, her brows knitted with the realization that the food they had shared for lunch amounted to three days' worth of this week's groceries. Waving heartily at her father's disappearing vehicle, Aly began figuring how much she'd have to cut back on her already meager meals until next week's paycheck.

~~~

"...the root cause was the malfeasance of male-female parenting..."

XXIII
PEOPLE'S HALL, 14:30

Dr. Brons was clearly fatigued. She recognized she'd have to seriously pace herself, if she were to have any real chance of getting through today's ordeal. "Mr. Ching, before the others return from their break, may I suggest that you and I take a brief respite, as well?" Without waiting for his reply, she turned away and, with head held regally aloof, stepped down to the nearby rest bench. As he followed her lead, Ching noted the Doctor's grace of motion – obviously a product of vintage theatrical training; hips and shoulders squared in perfectly alignment with her trim, athletic hips, and pelvis tilted slightly forward, which precluded any sluttish undulation in her stride. Such cultivated finesse and precision foot placement gave the onlooker a pleasant taste of refinement rarely seen in today's world. Ching found it markedly refreshing to witness this unusual display of captivating femininity and did not hide his admiration. Once seated, the old woman's aching body was instantly relieved. Ching slide onto the bench beside her.

While looking over the still vacant auditorium, she reached nimbly into her left vest pocket, extracted a handful of something, which she fed hastily into her mouth. The tension that had manifested itself at the corners of her pale, wizened lips instantly lifted, giving way to unmistakable ease.

"Doctor," Ching whispered playfully, "you do understand, don't you, that if that substance is what I think it is, I am obligated to inform the authorities?" She found his innocent, wide-eyed expression puzzling. Whether he was actually serious, or just toying with her, she was simply too tired to care one way or the other. The road had been so arduous and so very long, that whatever pecuniary action el Distrito might impose after today just didn't matter anymore. The only thing left that did matter was that she complete her mission and say what she had come to say. She took another pinch of something from her pocket and fed it to her trembling mouth. She knew better than to have deprived herself adequate nutrition throughout the day, but between this morning's deviancy permitting process and the non-stop confrontations at the dais, she had put aside any thoughts of food, out of shear necessity. Be that as it may, this snack had her feeling stronger now; good enough to get right back to work.

The recessed chronograph on the back wall reconfirmed that her authorized presentation time would soon end. "Do what you must do, my respected opponent, and I will do the same," she sniffed.

A few attending students had returning from the ordered break and were disinterestedly retaking their seats. The prolonged Rewards session had left them in an utter stupor; they were actually shuffling in, their vapid expressions looking moronic, void of any intelligent expression whatsoever. Under such an encumbered condition, the Doctor recognized that any hope she might have had that they would hear, understand, and engage themselves in her presentation was no longer reasonable; at least not until their compromised chemistry had restabilized itself. Perhaps Mr. Ching's relentless chiding had been an attempt to call her attention to that fact. However, be that as it may, what she now knew for certain was that she'd have to move forward and do so quickly.

The little time she had remaining demanded expediency. She decided to follow her instincts and believe that Ching was on her side; that he was someone she could trust to take in the relevance of her message and relay it to others who might understand the magnitude of its import. Yes! She would depend on Ching alone. Remaining seated, she drew in a deep, calming breath, and slowed squared her upper torso to him. Focusing directly onto his captivating grin, she began her uphill journey.

"Mr. Ching, it is well known that, male and female physicalities used to have greater distinguishing disparities than today. For instance, one athlete often had superior musculature over the other. That was due to a variety of reasons, but, more often than not, that superiority had been dictated by unsupervised genetics;

a fairly random outcome within the male-female family structure. Therefore, in order to adjust for this potentially discriminating outcome of their competition, el Distrito eliminated such dissimilarities between genders of that time. If I recall accurately, Mr. Ching, it was first decreed that all competitive standards be dropped entirely – in the "name of democratic fairness," is how the legislation read. Soon thereafter, biogenetics came into ..."

"Well, Doctor, that is precisely my point! The male gender group had been callously excluding others from competing physically by virtue of their inadequate masculine strength. Immensely unfair, was it not?"

"Well, Sir, if you mean females were excluded from male competition, then, no, it was not unfair. Not at all!"

"But, Dear, Dear Doctor, had it not been for corrective Distrito mandates, all other genders – those in addition to the female – would have also been precluded from athletic, as well as combat-readiness exercises along side males," he persisted. "Imagine, dear lady, how much fewer the number of unduly offended there would have been, had your generation simply acknowledged the full potential of every one of our genders!" Ching's eyes shot rapidly about the room, checking to see how their more energetic jousting was being reacted to by onlookers. Seeing no one displaying any comprehension of their talk, or anything else for that matter, he continued. "Why, Doctor, I'd be willing to wager that, but for you and I, no one here today has so much as an inkling of such an archaic sexist concept!"

"That would be a wager easily won, Mr. Ching, inasmuch as our audience was not even produced until decades following the correction."

"I'll also wager," he persisted, "it was for The People's enhanced general welfare that such societal correction was ordered. After all, the change had to be implemented if Distrito were ever to effectively stamp out the root cause of that hideous discrimination. Please don't shake your head so disapprovingly, Doctor. Our most erudite studies concluded that the root cause of such hurtful practices was the malfeasance of male-female parenting and the selfish Individualism it wrought. "

"Mr. Ching, with all due respect, my time is now severely limited! Let's get back to the subject at hand, shall we?"

~~~

"…she had reduced her Marlboro consumption just enough to afford the lay-away payments…"

XXIV
ALAN PROPERTIES

With proudly erect posture, Aly sat in readiness before his freshly polished walnut desk, enjoying the warming lemon scent of Endust. Poised for morning dictation, she held in her left hand, a narrow-lined green steno pad, and in her right, her most favored Schaeffer ink point pen. Impeccably groomed and donning her sharply pressed gabardine suite, Aly was the poster image of the professional administrative assistant. She had applied her makeup to perfection, using velvet black eyeliner for a seductive appeal, but the slightest hint of lip coloring, suggesting innocence. Her shining auburn hair was drawn back stylishly, fashioned in a meticulous French twist.

Aly's shapely legs were crossed modestly at her ankles, proudly displaying a pair of brand new four-inch, closed-toe patent leather heels. Over the past three weeks, she had reduced her Marlboro consumption just enough to afford the lay-away payments to Leeds shoe store. Smiling slightly, she replayed the well-earned satisfaction she had felt last Saturday, as she made out the final payment and liberated those gorgeous heels at the pickup window.

Having looked squarely into her boss' eyes, Aly had just finished asking his permission to periodically use the office copier for her own personal use. She had explained that, due to the long hours at this office, the nearby print shop was closed by the time she went home in the late evening, so using this copier would really be a help.

"Sure, Aly, that's fine. Feel free to use office postage, too, if need be. I know you won't abuse the privilege."

"Thank you, Mr. Alan. I don't expect to be needing either very often, but I'll be sure to keep a tally of what I use, and submit it to you as often as you like. I'll just add onto the list I already have going for the personal calls I make from my desk."

"That's fine, Aly," he answered. "I realize that's important to you, but please don't bother. Really. The quality of your work always exceeds my expectations, so, please don't pay me back. Just consider it an added thank-you for the excellent job you do for the company."

"Well, I hope you know that I would never take your generosity for granted, Sir, and really appreciate your vote of confidence. But, I do insist on keeping an on-going list of what I use, so we're both up to date on what I owe the company. It's only right, right? Anyway, if, at any time you want to see that tab, it'll be in my office desk in the middle right-hand drawer."

~~~

"It's quite astonishing, don't you think, Doctor, how everyone and everything are now truly equal?"

XXV
PEOPLE'S HALL, 14:47

As you wish, Doctor. However, before resuming your tedious subject matter – forgive my bluntness – I insist you indulge me a moment longer.

"Very well," she sighed wearily. "According to Distrito's archived database on Cultural Transformation, the implementation and enforcement of the Victimized Females Equality Act of our then-United States Code imposed a deluge of repressive restrictions on male behavior. According to that data, only federally-funded institutions were initially affected by that corrective engineering code, but that legislation eventually expanded into the current umbrella authority over all-gender interaction.

"What had been our country's highly esteemed standards of individual excellence for nearly 200 years were doggedly watered down to what all citizens must comply with today; an utter obsolescence of true competition. As I recall, first the prohibition of male-only competition occurred and then – within the short span of only two generations, the male's drive to excel in any arena had become nearly non-existent. All that needless devastation of the human spirit caused by surrendering, time and time again, to the endless demands of one complaining gender group after another. Such an unconscionable waste!" she added.

"My personal observation regarding such cultural abomination is that, in the earlier years, there had been an extraordinarily small number of qualified females who were physically capable of competing against those strengths historically characteristic of male physiology. Those females had not only been willing, but they were enthusiastic, as well, about the opportunity to compete against their male counterparts, according to traditionally-held male standards. Those young women never wanted male competitive standards to be lowered to a level that would be 'more achievable for all females.' But that had not been agreeable to a variety of powerful disgruntled We Fight For You groups, whose all-out revolts against the status quo were – to say the least – astonishing to witness. Whatever competitive or training goals were deemed to be physically out-of-reach for the average female athlete, those groups cried, 'Unfair!' or 'Sexist discrimination!' They wanted standards lowered to accommodate their limited abilities, as opposed to the young female athletes who simply wanted a chance to show their male counterparts they were up to the task of pure, unadulterated competition. But their wishes were ignored.

"First came the hue and cry on behalf of those females who were physiologically unable to compete against males of superior strength, endurance, and athletic talent. The We Fight For You and other victims' equality groups rejected the ardent cry of those female athletes who were capable of giving the young men a run for their money, so to speak. Instead, all male competitive standards across the board were lowered to accommodate all female physiological variables. There were many of us who fought on the side of performance excellence. Nevertheless, as history bears out, any counter arguments were overthrown; in the end, males were – and continue to be – forced to submit to ever-changing diluted norms."

"Aren't you forgetting the complaints of the other entitled minorities, Madam?"

"Ah, yes, the 'entitled minorities,'" she lamented. "There were so many – and each demanding rights that suited its own particular perceptions of equality. The Anti-masculinity Movement was destructive enough. But, then groups sprouted, found their political voices, and followed; those of different nationalities, skin colors, and physicalities. Why, even those barbaric terrorists..."

"Doctor! Look to the back wall! " he whispered sharply.

Moved by his obvious agitation, she obeyed and turned to look behind her. The monitor's glaring warning was pulsating frantically. Unimpressed, she turned back to face Ching.

"As I was saying, even those barbarians were assuaged by equality mediation. There was no attempt to protect the integrity of competition! No thoughts of qualifying standards for the individual! Only their own self-serving interest to penalize male athletes! I thought that incessant squabbling would never cease. Did you, Mr. Ching?"

He had tried to warn her, but she was intent upon proceeding without caution, it would seem. He grinned approvingly. "Well, Doctor, you are certainly expounding on a time before my own. Nonetheless, I am sufficiently knowledgeable about that historic period to safely add that, every one of those contentious groups was awarded its demands, and yet not one remained satisfied.

"On the positive side, however, I'd say the Victimized Females Equality Act was greatly successful in rectifying any perception of disparity; once all male-only sporting and athletic events were officially banned and uniformly replaced by female-male events, that is. After that, things became relatively peaceful. Both genders had come to be seen as complete equals. No disparaging judgements or assessments of qualifying worthiness were allowed. Consequently, no arguments could be made for or against it. It may have taken a number of generations to engineer, but now such contention no longer exists.

"It was the subsequent Mandate for All-gender Interaction that generated today's prevailing harmony, if I remember my history correctly; the 'unlimited activities among all citizens without one gender group's cruel ostracizing of another, whether based on dissimilar tastes, needs, aspirations, or perceived capabilities.' It's quite astonishing, really, don't you think, Doctor, how everyone and everything are now truly equal? No longer is any citizen subjected to the humiliation of competitive defeat, or the embarrassment of being replaced by someone deemed better qualified for any given undertaking. The core cause of that damaging humiliation has been expelled from The People's cultural consciousness. Doctor," he added enthusiastically, "they don't even understand the corrosive concept of selfishness! Why, from their earliest experience, our youth products are indelibly impressed with the new reality! *'Distrito provides because we deserve it.'* That says it all, doesn't it, Doctor?"

"Well, not quite," she said dismayed. "That initial social engineering was targeted to accommodate the female so-called 'minority' and its complaints of discriminatory standards in athletic events. That might have appeared at the time to be a benign adjustment, but as with any fungal invasion, that engineering metamorphosed into an infection of both genders, as well as any interaction that was based on traditional concepts. It infected not only female-male differences, but also broke down any and all defining parameters for every one of the protected genders. It was that very engineering maneuver that ultimately obliterated all previously-held cultural standards. In due course, its contamination infiltrated our school yards, military, and academia, too. Standard protocols of civility, as well as academic proficiency, athletic competence and strength, combat readiness, social units, why – freedom of expression overall - were sacrificed for el Distrito's micromanagement and eventual criminalization of any display of individual pursuit whatsoever."

The Doctor leaned forward and grabbed an old, discolored thermos she had placed earlier at the leg of the bench where she sat. Not giving a gnat's hoot that her verbal transgressions were forbidden, she nonchalantly raised the container to her lips, and swiftly downed three thirst-quenching gulps. Briskly recapping the container and setting it back onto the floor, she pressed her eyelids together for a stolen moment of solace. *"So there!" she muttered to herself. "If they expect me to participate in their decadent Rewards rituals and God-knows-what-kind of other debauchery, they can think again!"* She then reopened her eyes, relieved to be feeling somewhat refreshed. Her wrists were beginning to throb, though. Something she'd have to see to later after her lecture today.

Ching had been watching her with total wonder. *"Such a proud and self-sufficient woman,"* he chuckled. *"One who shows more endurance than someone a fraction her age!"*

"Mr. Ching," she continued, that piece of social engineering was intentionally targeted to degrade masculine spirit."

"Of course, Doctor! And it was the right and fair thing to do, was it not?" he prodded.

"In order to ascertain fairness, objective evaluation, rather than subjectivity, is required," she countered. "I understand I'm the only one here who actually witnessed those horrid transformations, so I'll tell you this: such acquiescence to the demands of those unqualified was particularly punitive to our males. It was particularly damaging to our talented young men who had studied and trained so strenuously. Theirs was an unwavering dedication toward reaching astounding competitive excellence. All their hard work disregarded for the sake of 'class rights'," she said wistfully.

"Well, Doctor, in hindsight we know that it was those earlier fairness challenges that led to a multitude of doors opening for those less fortunate. Today, a more equalized justice prevails; no one – no matter their gender or color, no matter how ill-equipped, incapacitated, or unfortunate that they might have been unfairly judged by earlier standards – may be excluded from any undertaking whatsoever. Don't you find that just?"

"No, Mr. Ching, I most certainly do not," she sighed.

~~~

"Why should my employer be penalized because I cannot or will not come to work and earn my pay?"

XXVI
ENTERPRISING EXCELLENCE, 4 ATT

She rose in the black stillness of pre-dawn hours to prepare for her day. How delicious it was to rethink and often reprioritize the pressing tasks at hand that were carried over from yesterday. Her years of expertise provided her with an unshakeable confidence that her personal orchestration always ensured the successful completion of targeted goals. "Excellence is in the details," she'd whisper smiling, taking a seat at her well-ordered desk.

It had been a wondrous fifteen years, building her own business on her "own sweat," as her father used to say. Today she didn't expect to accomplish much – if any – constructive work. The three neatly-piled stacks of city-, county-, and state-mandated reports assured her of that. Beginning with her professional experience as a 17-year-old stenographer, the Doctor had learned that mandated government reports were not to be taken lightly. In today's world, the savvy entrepreneur understood that even a hint of non-compliance could bring swift and painful pecuniary retaliation – a retaliation so debilitating it could easily force her to shut her doors. "The cost of doing business," she sighed, adjusting her reading glasses at the bridge of her nose to read the fine print of reporting instructions.

Suzanne stepped punctually into her office at 07:30. "Good morning, Doctor!" her musical greeting rang out. Before the Doctor could respond, the young secretary sat down, modestly crossing her legs to her left side. While brushing imaginary creases from her Irish linen skirt, the girl studied the orderly stacks of paperwork that would be requiring her attention. She then poised her steno pad and pen, signaling her readiness for the morning's dictation.

This employee did her best to mirror her employer's image; both were meticulously groomed and sat with impeccable posture. Suzanne so revered the Doctor, that she took great care to emulate her mentor's professionalism in every way. She loved working for Enterprising Excellence, and was ever so proud to be her trusted office manager.

Suzanne's so-called peers couldn't begin to understand, much less appreciate, the sterling standards of honour the Doctor and her enterprise were all about. "You mean you actually like going to work for that uptight witch?" they'd ask, bewildered. Suzanne saw their little minds as being absurdly juvenile; they couldn't begin to understand the basic concept of conducting honourable work through integrity! Why, the fact that she refused to take her accumulated paid sick days rendered her crazy in their minds. She just couldn't get them to agree that one should never ask to be paid for work they have not done.

"Why should my employer be penalized because I cannot or will not come to work and earn my pay?" she had asked the receptionist from across the hall. "If you were the Doctor, would you pay me your hard-earned money for staying home, rather than going into the office on a work day?"

"Of course not! Why should I? You haven't done anything for me!" was the girl's snappy retort.

"Exactly my point," Suzanne replied simply.

"And a hearty top-o-the morn' to you, Suzanne! You look as sharp as usual, you clever girl, you! Let's tackle the ADA's diktat of the day; that one that commands our hiring of that blind woman to be your assistant. OK with you?"

"Absolutely, Doctor!" she answered efficiently. "Honestly, though, being distracted by that woman and her seeing-eye dog just makes me angry. They're only going to make it harder for us to get our work done, you know? Not being able to hire someone who can actually take some of this work off our shoulders, keeps me up at night!"

"So," she said obliviously, "what do you calculate the so-called 'reasonable accommodation' for our new office worker will cost us, Suzanne? Have you had a chance to get to those figures?"

"You bet I have!" she said, all revved up. "In addition to the so-called 'enhanced work station,' the expense for her new computer's

magnification module is beyond belief. I mean, that module alone will add another $17,000 to our initial out-of-pocket!"

"And we don't even know whether she's skilled enough to do even basic clerical support functions, do we?" the Doctor replied.

"That's right! But, according to the ADA's fine print, applicants don't have to be skilled, only 'willing to learn new business concepts and staff practices'. God, Doctor! Why the heck did our so-called government representatives ever put this policy into law? Don't they know how destructive it is to business?"

"But, Suzanne, you know full well that the average government representative only looks out for himself, and he does that by ensuring the furtherance of his own power. The government gets to pocket a portion of those paid 'accommodations.' That revenue is power. And with power come the goodies, right? And, after all," she added sarcastically, "they must show good faith to their financial backers by hog-tying us, the ones who provide the jobs..."

~~~

"...to determine that the patriarchal family had no redeeming value in our society was absolutely wrong!"

XXVII
PEOPLE'S HALL, 15:06

"Be that as it may, Mr. Ching," she heard her voice ringing, "I believe you've said all you need to about this matter. Now, really! I absolutely insist you withhold further comment and allow me to continue with my presentation." She paused, expecting a sarcastic remark. Hearing none, she felt free to continue. Reaching again for her thermos, she looked over the auditorium and was surprised, as well as delighted, to see that the all the seats appeared to be again occupied. The students' return sparked renewed hope for her success today. As the Doctor placed the cool stainless steel mouth of the thermos to her lips, sharp, burning pains shot through her wrists, so she hurriedly took a large swig of cool water. Once she placed the thermos back on the floor, the stress to her wrist joints had been removed and those pains immediately stopped. She then stood up, squared her shoulders proudly, and stepped with confidence to the awaiting dais. How it gladdened her heart to see those young faces before her! *"Fruition begins with but one seed,"* she thought encouragingly.

"Welcome back, Citizens! I am so pleased you've decided to rejoin us," she said warmly. "Mr. Ching and I have been sharing historical accounts," she smiled. "You're just in time to hear my explanation of the importance of a two-gender society. Those of you who are looking at me a bit perplexed, I ask that you listen and listen well: Simply because the knowledge of the existence of this country's earlier two-gender society has been withheld from you does not nullify its existence in any way. Also, that society indelibly enriched the civility and honour of our people for many, many generations. Yes, that, indeed, is a fact and, as such, it cannot be erased from history simply because you have not been made aware of it."

"Nor does your foolish disregard of Distrito's gender speech guidelines ensure your desired achievement with this audience," Ching whispered conspiratorially from behind her.

She instantly spun around and faced him. "Enough!" she hissed between clenched teeth. Then, without as much as a pause, she smoothly pivoted back to face the students. "The mandate to which Mr. Ching refers," she explained softly," eradicated our traditional two-gender culture and that eradication is exactly what I've come here today to challenge. You students simply *must* be made to understand that the enactment of that mandate officially abolished..."

"And just why 'must' they be made to understand, my esteemed Doctor?" he challenged. "Those here who wish to make sense of your words are certainly free to tune in. But, for now, please explain this to me – to all of us, again... why must these students be made to understand a cultural transformation that occurred generations before their time?" He had resumed standing by her side, looking questioningly into her soft hazel eyes.

Ching's intentions were all too clear to her; he was being purposely argumentative to disrupt her presentation. All afternoon he'd been distracting her; keeping her from completing her goal. No, she now realized that he wasn't simply stimulating an intellectual exchange, but, rather, undermining any progress with the audience she had hoped to make. She looked to the floor for a moment to gather her thoughts, and then looked into his eyes. His gaze displayed only fondness.

"If you'll allow me to proceed, Sir, your question will be answered in due course," she muttered disdainfully. "As I was saying," she said to her audience, "the Ultimate Sustainment Act of 2037 was, essentially, the final blow to our then-country's all-but-gasping family structure. After the government's total disempowerment of the traditional family, what followed was the regulated infantalization of The People. The authors of the Act were, indeed, clever; its implementation was so comprehensive and brilliantly executed that the dissolution of the nuclear family eventually eroded into collapse. I say to you here and now that for our government to have determined that the patriarchal family had no redeeming value in our society was absolutely wrong! Why, when I think of the grave injustice to our children..."

The sudden screech was bone-piercing. The old woman's heart sank. *"Oh, no!" she thought. "Again I've said too much too quickly."* She looked up, fully expecting to see a BCI enforcer coming to apprehend her. Her beleaguered heart was racing now, pounding under the assault of each high-pitched, deafening squeal. The room became dark and began to spin. When the alarm abruptly ceased, she was lying limply on the floor.

~~~

"If I don't keep my word, I am worthless..."

XXVIII
MOVING ON

She always enjoyed running Friday errands. The walks represented a brief time out from the quarterly bustle at Alan Properties. In particular, it was a welcomed opportunity to mentally review her scheduled projects for the day.

This morning she had brought a blank company check to purchase office postage for the month. Today marked the tenth day following the close of another fiscal quarter. This meant that she and the full-charge bookkeeper were set to spend the upcoming weekend at the office to ensure the investors received their quarterlies in a timely manner.

All of yesterday afternoon and then for three hours earlier today, Mr. Alan, as general partner, had dictated to her the blanket narratives to the limited partners of all thirty-two property investment groups. The narratives consisted of explanatory notes for the numbers reflected on each investment property's P&L statement, as well as Mr. Alan's subjective projections for each asset. Once Aly finished transcribing those shorthand notes, she took great professional pride making certain that all documents in the final packages were error-free and collated perfectly before presenting them to her employer for final review and signature. Once Mr. Alan signed off on those packages, she and the bookkeeper had the go-ahead to mail them out.

It was always satisfying to find that huge pile of signed reports on her desk when she got back from running errands. Not so satisfying, however, were those occasions when she'd find a scribbled note from her boss, paper clipped to this or that page, instructing her to change his narrative in some way. Although those changes usually involved only an aesthetic adjustment, retyping the page from scratch and returning it for signature 'right away' was time-consuming; an irritating delay that could have been avoided had she better anticipated those adjustments and taken the extra steps to avoid them . Such irritations were slight and very short-lived, though, for they paled in light of the resulting meticulously accurate, well formatted, truly outstanding publications.

Aly enjoyed the fact that her employer was tolerant of many human foibles, but strictly demanded excellence in her work performance. "Hold yourself responsible for a higher standard than anybody expects of you. Never excuse yourself!" he would chant. "I read that Henry Ward Beecher quote in high school, Aly, and it just stuck with me. That mindset has served me and this business extremely well over the years." She smiled lazily, as her thoughts strayed to the weekend project ahead. It was another opportunity for her to excel.

~~~

Aly was enchanted to see the elderly couple strolling ahead of her on the boulevard sidewalk. The woman's frail hand was gracefully holding the crook of her companion's arm, seemingly indifferent to others about them. Each was dressed conservatively; both donned a well-tailored three-quarter length linen top coat, stylish hat, and gloves; he strutted ceremoniously with an elegantly crafted walking stick.

He, obviously a gentleman, walked on the traffic side of his woman. This was an action that symbolized his wish to protect her from possible danger. Aly recalled that this had been a common practice for earlier generations, but was rarely seen anymore. Most contemporary women had already claimed We Fight For You superiority over their men, rejecting such courtesies as "offering their arm" to a woman while walking together, opening a door for his female companion, standing up when she entered the room, and so on. It was somehow reassuring to see the couple's gentile respect for each other. It gave her joy to witness such traditionalized doting that had years before been accepted – and welcomed – behavior. Her thoughts were interrupted as the old woman broke out in a delightfully light-hearted laugh. Aly looked up to find her pointing to something across the street. "Remember, Dear, when your folks had their mercantile shop over there?" At that point, Aly had reached the staircase leading from the street to the second-story office. She ascended each step slowly, wanting to savor that most agreeable display of civility.

~~~

It had been a trying, but invigorating twelve years. Working for Mr. Alan had always been an intellectual challenge. Each new property acquisition package brought to her desk required that she study and understand thoroughly all contractual terms of the investment, as well as its financial obligations. As asset manager, she was responsible for implementing and enforcing those terms, as well as accommodating the idiosyncrasies of each new group of limited partners. Mr. Alan's direction had been personally and professionally edifying. The oft-times strenuous learning curves allowed her to build well-honed business proficiencies, as well as fortify her self-confidence. Aly knew she was capable of moving on now. She felt more than ready to be challenged outside the familiar sphere of Alan Properties.

She greeted him respectfully and sat down in front of his richly polished desk. He sat as a proud and authoritative figure in his beautiful leather upholstered executive arm chair, his eyes smiling warmly. "I never thought I'd have a 'last day' here," she mused silently. Because Mr. Alan was not a man to waste his or anyone else's time, she immediately reached across his neatly categorized project folders and handed him her well-worn employment file. An "Exit Checklist" was neatly clipped at the top.

Over his granny reading glasses, he efficiently scanned the checklist from top to bottom, where he paused at the bottom line. "What's this 'Employee to Reimburse Employer' figure, Aly?"

"It's what I owe you for the company's supplies and equipment I've made personal use of over the last few years, Sir," she answered.

"Ah, yes! I remember that vaguely, but surely you don't expect me to hold you to that agreement. You have been worth your weight in gold to me, Aly. It doesn't seem right that you should leave here owing me money, when, after all these years, I am the one who is your debt. You are really something, Kiddo," he added. "It took a lot of stamps, paper copies, and phone calls to amount to this much money!" Her employer stood up and leaned across the desk, handing the file back to her. "Here. Just have the bookkeeper cut your final check for your full amount and that's the final word."

"With all due respect, Sir, you and I entered into a business agreement and I'm asking you to respect me enough to allow me to honour it." Both standing, their eyes locked. His were shining with approval; hers with determination. "Mr. Alan, I've already made out my check to you," she announced proudly, as she handed him her neatly typed personal check for $1,432.07.

"Oh, Aly! Aly! I could always count on you to do the right thing. But, this is really going to cut into your final paycheck, isn't it? I mean, I really wish you would reconsider and just forget about paying this back. Really I do."

She stood up, offered him her hand and said, "If there's one thing I've learned, Sir, it's this: If I don't keep my word, I am worthless, and certainly no longer worthy of your respect. This payment to you keeps our slate clean and allows me to walk out of here with dignity."

Holding her gaze warmly, he took her hand in both of his and squeezed firmly. "Thank you for a wonderful twelve years, Aly." Glowing with personal pride, Aly turned and left his office, quietly closing the door behind her.

~~~

"Surely…you're capable of understanding that Ozzie and Harriet don't live here anymore!"

XXIX
PEOPLE'S HALL, 15:33

In a fog of semi-consciousness, the Doctor hears muted discourse. She recognizes the simulated voice of the argumentative dark-skinned female, who had challenged her earlier. The young woman was incensed and making a heated demand that she, "la idiota," be removed. 'This disgusting Remnant should be taken away and punished for acts of heterosexism!" she shouted. With his usual diplomacy, Ching was trying his best to appease.

"This is simply an exercise, Salinas Sector 2. In total fairness, the old Remnant has certainly reminded us of that today. So, really, there is no reason to become so recklessly angered, is there? Perhaps you should consider indulging yourself in another Rewards pause? This day has, more than likely, been extremely stressful to so many, so it would be understandable if you were to decide to leave us in order to do so."

The old woman realized that Ching was cradling her head on his lap. She reached up and lightly tapped his forearm. He looked down at her with a genuinely happy smile. "Ah! Dear Lady, you have returned to us! Are you feeling well enough to continue, or shall we call it a day, so to speak?"

"I'd like to continue... while I still have time," she answered weakly.

"Please take this, Doctor. It will fortify you." Trustingly, she accepted the textured blue tablet, and then drank from the beverage package he'd carefully placed to her lips. The substance was familiar and comforting. She looked up to her gallant protector, her face brightened with gladness.

"Mr. Ching, help me up. Please. I'd like to finish the task at hand." At that, he helped her to a sitting position and then stood himself. With gentle deference, he grasped her hand firmly and helped her to her feet. In this process, she took the opportunity to glance over his physique. *"Good Lord! I haven't seen such a beautiful male specimen since...how long has it been, anyway?"* she asked herself. *"He puts me to mind of someone, but I can't quite put my finger on it,"* she sighed resignedly. *"No matter! This fine-looking Tigres wouldn't have stood a chance with the much younger me!"* As though reading her thoughts, his mouth curved widely into an invitingly impish grin. Supporting the Doctor under her left elbow and waist, they swiveled around in perfect unison to face the audience, each very much aware of their dangerously patrician manner. Unperturbed by this reality, Ching escorted his charge with respectful care back to the awaiting dais, halting precisely on the speaker's mark.

Ching spoke first. "Citizens, as you can see, our featured speaker has returned to complete her presentation. The Doctor has only a short time remaining to do so. So, to help her with what is now required brevity, the Doctor and I will continue the poignant exchange we were having while you were still enjoying your last break." Turning to her, he asked, "All right with you, Fair Lady?"

This pre-emption at her podium took her aback. She had not expected such blatant rudeness from Ching. Looking squarely to the audience, she answered, "Not at all, Mister Ching. Your participation today has been most helpful."

"I'm pleased to hear you say that, Doctor. As you may recall, we were speaking of a long-ago era before male aggression had been genetically eliminated. I was pointing out to you that, for your generation, such aggression against family members and others had been widely accepted. Looking back, one could find it quite understandable that such aggression lead to our earlier culture's practice of the brutalization and unjust treatment of all genders."

"Yes! That's what I'm protesting!" yelled the aberrantly dark-skinned woman. "As a just people, we know sexist males showed others how vile their dominance was. They were horrid to females, males, and female children; and, really, to anyone who fought against their sexist cruelties. Our praise to el Distrito for defanging those monsters! Now you, high and mighty Doctor, tell us that male-dominated family units were good. Mentiras!

You don't have the right to spew such lies!" Throwing up her well-toned, stocky arms in exasperation, she stomped up the aisle and out the nearby exit. In her wake was an awkward stillness, marked only by the monitor's incessant pulsations.

Unmoved by the woman's angry outbreak, the Doctor continued. "Mr. Ching, the brutalization of others was not a characteristic peculiar to the male gender; rather, it was a symptom of inadequate childhood conditioning necessary to prepare children for the responsibilities of mature adulthood. Brutalization is, more precisely, the most unfortunate result of the lack of moral instruction needed to effect the virtue of strong personal integrity. Let's not forget, Mr. Ching, that case studies at that time reflected a preponderance of violent acts committed by females against their family members, when compared to those of males. Actually, it was not that long ago when our country witnessed female aggression escalate to the intentional maiming and killing of their own innocent offspring and unborn. This was occurring while the male, or father, of those children was fulfilling his designated role of provider. You remember, don't you, Mr. Ching, when the provider, as head of the family, assumed the obligations of working to earn a living; a living that 'put a roof over' his family's head and 'food in their bellies' – as the saying went?" she prodded.

"Doctor," he said impatiently, "as your then-United States Supreme Court upheld, those studies served to verify the argument that those violent female acts were an involuntary outpouring of male aggression. It is well known that females, per se, are not at all aggressive and that their rare displays of aggression were effectively due to aberrant mitotic cell division. It had become clear to el Distrito that once the stem cell mitosis process was re-engineered – partly through microencapsulation - the male's predilection toward aggression was easily remedied. And, since we also had cell-substrate technology at our disposal, it was a simple matter to achieve asexual equality for all by way of regulating stem cell differentiation. So, Dear Doctor, I'm sure you can see how this haploidic achievement really trumps your illogical pursuit to reinstitute the patriarchal family. Correct? Surely, even with your advanced age," he sneered, "you're capable of understanding that Ozzie and Harriet do not live here anymore!" Miffed by her silence, he prodded, "Are you *not*, Madam Remnant?"

His betrayal was disgusting. What she had perceived to be his captivating charm was now gone. In its place loomed the unmistakable, very real, presence of evil. She felt its threat lodging in her throat, while her wrists burned with intensifying pain. Angrily, she clenched her strong, liver-spotted hands into fists of defiance. *"How utterly stupid I've been to believe I could trust him!"* "No, Mr. Ching," her voice rang out. "As was Judas, you, too, are despicable, as well as dead wrong!"

~~~

The entire Hall reverberated with vehement chants as the BC Officer scurried breathlessly down the aisle, his white iridescent robe flowing as dramatically as a vampire's kingly cape. He stopped abruptly, hands on hips, and shook his head with consternation. "Of all the permit infractions," he hissed, "the Sector would never have anticipated such an inexcusable violation from you, Dr. Brons!"

"Oh? To which violation do you refer, Officer?" she asked innocently.

"Well, it's the violation of Global Edict 1320, as if you didn't know!" his motionless lips replied.

"But, Officer, I and my worthy opponent here," she pointed to Ching at her right, "were simply discussing the historical precepts that existed prior to present day law. Since this is an academic setting, and my goal as an educator is to stimulate the students' faculties of reason, I simply premised my statements with a few societal norms of earlier times. That certainly is not a violation of my permit, is it? After all," she prompted, "my intention is not to incite, but to instruct."

"Nevertheless, Doctor," he persisted sternly, "you have committed a grievous hate crime during this so-called exercise; a crime in which you pledged to never engage."

"You are completely wrong in your conclusion, Officer," she persisted. This debate has been energetic, but certainly not unlawful. Don't you agree, Mister Ching?" She pivoted toward her challenger, expecting to see his nod of assent. Instead, he faced away, as though to avoid contamination.

"Doctor, I hereby accuse you of heinous heterosexism," proclaimed the BC Officer. "On behalf of el Distrito, we command you to appear before el Distrito Tribunal three days hence at the hour of Primary Infusion. In deference to your age and prior standing in the Sector, you will be allowed to complete the time remaining on your Permit for this presentation. However, should you repeat your vile sexist speech at any time between now and the moment of permit expiration, orders are already in place for your immediate and final removal from this Hall. Is that understood, Doctor?"

She heard his digitized words without interest. *"How odd to see his still lips at the very moment I hear him speak," she marveled.*

"Doctor, I asked you a question!" his steely voice threatened.

"Oh, I'm sorry, Officer. But, for some reason, your words did not properly transmute. Would you kindly repeat your question?" Her focus remained on his straining, motionless mouth.

"You are prohibited from repeating your sexist statements. You are to submit to Tribunal Inquiry three days hence. *Do* you or *do* you *not* understand, Doctor?"

"I do," she muttered absently. Apparently satisfied, the man turned wordlessly, and strode away.

~~~

"…the Movement had to employ political muscle to forcibly emasculate them."

XXX
PEOPLE'S HALL, 16:14

"Doctor, your persistent efforts to revive the so-called 'traditional' family structure have become tedious," said Ching. "Frankly, it was a cultural more of your time, not today's. Besides, even if you could convince The People of its importance in some existential way, the gender distinctions needed to comprise such a societal unit are now chemically circumvented immediately after germination. It's simply the new order of things. You know this as well as I, Doctor," he added with emphasis.

She flinched at the mention of "germination" rather than "conception." Was there no other in this room who was following – actually hearing and understanding - her intended message? If there were but one, this exercise in seeming futility will not have been in vane. "But, we were speaking of the importance of that family structure, Mr. Ching. Certainly my permit allows us to continue our debate for the time remaining, doesn't it?"

"Doctor, what is the point? Really?" he asked, gesturing to an auditorium that was now completely absent of attendees.

"Oh, I am unable to answer that precisely, Sir. Nevertheless, I would be irresponsible as a scheduled speaker not to complete this session up to and through the time allotted. Even though our audience seems to have deserted us, we could continue with an entertaining joust of opposing philosophies; express ourselves fully." His eyes brightened with intrigue. "What do you say, Mr. Ching?" she asked in full challenge.

"Dear Lady, by all means," he replied softly.

"We were debating the matter of male aggression and you stated that it became necessary to eradicate that gender all together for the good of the People. Am I correct?" He nodded respectfully.

"Very well, then," she continued, "I will jump right in and counter that premise by emphasizing that our country's institution of the paternal family was coveted by the world for centuries. And this was so in my lifetime. The male was the dominant, securing element of the unit, who protected his female wife. In return, the female wife was obligated to provide him with a secure, orderly home, and legitimate heirs. In return for that security, the woman was freed from giving birth indiscriminately to out-of-wedlock children and having to fend for herself and those illegitimate offspring to, at best, eek out the barest, most meager, and often, demeaning and dangerous existence. Prior to legitimatizing their relationship with the protection of marriage, there had been no sustainable quality of life beyond which women could hope to excel."

"But, being dominated and often savagely mistreated by those authoritative males was the extremely high price females and their children had to pay for their so-called 'protection,'" he countered.

"All heads of families were not unkind bullies, Mr. Ching."

"Yes, but the brutes who did commit such heartless acts far outnumbered those who did not."

"Mr. Ching," she said impatiently, "that is simply untrue. Any educated (and, yes, I do mean pre-Distrito-indoctrinated) person of that time knew full well that those brutes were a product of either a mental imbalance, or lack of good character resulting from an uncivilized upbringing. Such Cretans – if I may – were often products of unwed mothers, who failed to provide their offspring with the crucial influence of a strong, loving father; a decent, responsible father whom a male child could hope to emulate as an adult, and by whose example a female child could formulate her preferences for a future mate.

"'Upbringing' is certainly a misnomer on my part, for those malcontented children really had none; rather, they grew up having less supervision than that given lower mammals. Anyway, good men were essential to the family equation, and there were many. They taught by example how to honour - even revere – their mothers and sisters, as well as respect and protect any and all females outside the family unit. Protecting a woman and respecting her status as another man's wife or daughter were sacrosanct. And believe me," she added wistfully, "it was a beautiful thing to bask in the security of male devotion. This masculine teaching was rigidly reinforced by stern disciplinary action. Dishonourable behavior was often met with societal shunning. Mr. Ching, our country's cultural institution – the one that generated far more decent, honourable, and productive individuals than not – would not have been possible without strong male-female family units that practiced healthy paternalism."

"That thesis became outmoded long ago, Doctor. As a matter of fact, it's only been two generations or so since the then-We Fight For You Movement clearly established that male participation was non-essential to childrearing; that it is the female who is endowed with its gender-specific characteristics of fairness, sensitivity, and all-inclusiveness. Of course, because males staunchly defended the imagined nobility of traditional America, the Movement had to employ political muscle to forcibly emasculate them. It was the only way to effect the changes that have dramatically reformed us as The People."

"But, those changes were neither constructive for our country, nor its individuals. Why, they merely served to destroy a most proud citizenry and its dedication to honour, duty, and individual excellence," she countered.

"And Distrito would agree that its targeted goal was just that. Look!" he added in exasperation, "to point out the obvious, since your 18th Century, our country was both politically and culturally fractured about matters that were based in gender equality. The obvious solution was to put an end to such pernicious gender discrimination and the incessant discussion that gave it energy."

"What, again, I ask you, is the 'discrimination' to which you repeatedly refer, Mr. Ching? If you are again referring to the abuses within a few traditional families, I still believe it was ludicrous to dismantle the nurturing family, rather than correct the individuals who committed those abuses."

"Actually, Doctor, I am now referring to discrimination against individual gender choice that barred individuals from being who and what they wished, rather than endure the cruelty of random biological circumstances your Nature had dealt them and to which they remained restricted. Yes, I am speaking of those who were born physiologically male, but wished to become female, or visa versa; those who wished for the versatility of carrying both male as well as female genitalia, but were refused that choice by a scornful traditional society; those who were precluded from marrying whom and what they wished, and those who simply wished the freedom to choose those with whom they wished to practice and enjoy their chosen sexual diversions."

"You sound like a proponent of those views," she murmured disdainfully.

He bristled ever so slightly. "Do I? If you think that, then we are wasting precious permit time, aren't we, Doctor? What I am trying so hard to do is help you quickly reconstruct that series of events that led to our well-regulated and smooth-functioning society of today. As is readily clear to anyone caring enough to take notice, dissatisfaction no longer exists; Distrito insulates The People from unjust treatment shamelessly doled out by others. I am referring to our earlier point of conjecture; namely, competition.

"Since its eradication first from our children's schooling and later from the workplace, The People have had less need for the male predilection to compete, prove strength, and lord power over others. Concurrent with that societal cleansing, the expansion of gender categories was implemented to include the realization of whatever one wished to experience. El Distrito made certain anything and everything was for the taking; those who had been victimized had only to ask for appellate relief. Since the High Tribunal's decision that these options were mere extensions of their entitlement of Freedom of Unhampered Expression.

The People have had no wish to be bothered with your pesky references to inconsequential cultural events. You somehow have this fallacious notion that, if you could only impart 'the truth' and the People would consider that truth, you will have won another shot at reversing present-day norms. My challenge to you is this, Dear Doctor: With Distrito providing lives of complete fulfillment, made possible by gender cleansing and the infinite and immediate supply of fulfilled need and desires, why would The People want to throw that away for your silly notion of tradition? Please, Doctor, tell me – tell the DRI - why you even bother!"

His attack was starkly wounding. "Is it so inappropriate, Mr. Ching? Is reversal too much to hope and work for? Is my fervent wish to promote and praise individual achievement and lofty character beyond possibility?" she asked. "Despite your opposition, I simply will not believe this pretense of yours. Others may be misled by it, but I am not and I refuse to be! Why, the stakes are simply too severe! We simply must change things. You know full well what is risked if we refuse to do so." Then, in a whisper, "Please, please, Mr. Ching, won't you *please* stop this charade and help me get this done?" she implored. "I know you're a kindred soul, I just *know* it, she whispered ardently. Please, oh, *please* tell these people how it will benefit them to consider others' philosophies. Even those of a fading Remnant! If they could only see that you support..."

~~~

After Aly's home had been seized, she no longer bore the reviled mark of "landowner."

XXXI
FREEDOM TO CHOOSE, 21 ATT

It was nearly midnight. Sometime within the next two minutes the sector's local Enforcement Unit would begin making its rounds. The young woman peered cautiously into the blackness of the alleyway, first looking to her right and then to the left. Chancing that the moment was safe, she hurriedly patted down the bags of contraband, flattening them against her lean torso. With open palms, she made the final swipes to smooth the surface of her London Fogger. Now satisfied that tonight's purchases would not visually detectable, Aly stepped into the beckoning darkness.

The direct route would get her home in a quarter of an hour, but that would be tempting Fate just a tad too much, so she opted, instead, to return amidst the decaying warehouses. After so many years of sneaking to meet procurers, she had grown to trust the dank furrows amidst decomposing rubble to guide her safely back from those clandestine meetings. Although more menacing, these rutted pathways had always guided her back home, presumably undetected, within 23 minutes flat.

One hour later, Aly sat in the comfort of her kitchen, cupping her hands carefully around a warm bowl of contraband. Smiling dreamily, she leisurely savored each spoonful of the life-sustaining mash, while simultaneously giving thanks for tonight's bounty. With eyes closed, Aly concentrated on prolonging the visceral pleasure of this illegal ingestion. The haunting question was how much longer she'd be able to continue the pickups without detection. If she were ever again caught procuring, the imposition of interspecies inoculation would be immediate. If there were one more misconduct charge imposed against her, Distrito's pending Writ of Execution would be re-activated, ensuring this pickup would be her last. She cringed to think that, once her immune system was seized by those contaminants, her body's immediate metabolic response would be its convulsive rejection of any and all probiotic nutrients; it would leave her physiologically compelled to take in only Distrito-approved compounds. Finally, her inherent capacity to effectively maintain her own health would be challenged, and her independent occupancy status denied. Without the authority to live alone, one was always assigned to the Final Compound.

Pursuant to The People's Property Equalization Act, Aly's family home had been duly confiscated and she was subsequently assigned a living compartment in a nearby resident module. Although it provided little more than bare essentials, she found it sufficiently utilitarian with space enough to meet her Spartan needs. The transparency of this new location had been a crippling drawback, though, as conducting surveillance of her comings and goings was much easier for them now. It made her ability to move about "under the radar" cumbersome, and the required advance planning of her pickups especially time-consuming.

After Aly's home was seized, she no longer bore the reviled mark of "landowner." On the other hand, because of her obstinate refusal to desist from her decades-long crusade to revive practices of personal dignity, she received the tribunal's order to register as an Admitted Individualist. It was that damning designation that had triggered around-the-clock scrutiny of Aly's personal and professional activities. However, she trusted that, because she had voluntarily registered as a self-proclaimed Remnant, she would be allowed open-ended deferment from compulsory implantation of a Caring Locator & Status Assessment chip.

Closing her fatigued eyes, she luxuriated in the moment, giving thanks for her good fortune. "It's been a grand day," she thought with a smile.

~~~

"...undertaking a live birth would have been met with swift imprisonment and surgical correction."

XXXII
UNMASKED

Her head was pounding unmercifully. No matter; she must finish the message. Squeezing her eyelids tightly, the Doctor managed to partially clear her blurred vision. Having regained some clarity, she no longer saw The People's Hall, but the confines of her small, Spartan module. She blinked hard and slowly. No change. Once again. Still no change. It has to be the crushing headache creating this illusion. But, as quickly as that thought registered, she realized that, although she had no memory of leaving the Hall and returning to her compartment, she did distinctly recall asking her exasperating opponent for help. *"Yes, now I remember feeling faint,"* she thought, regaining some composure. "Well, my lecture permit has obviously expired," she spoke aloud.

He was sitting next to her, gently holding her hand in his, as she lay on the Sector-issued day bed. His presence was wonderfully comforting, as was the firmness of his grasp. The Doctor was feeling what her grandmother used to describe as "bone tired," a weakness that had enveloped her unnoticed. She felt a creeping sense of resignation, but quickly brushed it aside. "I see you're still with me, my friend! Why might that be?" she asked.

Her voice started him into quickly releasing her hand and jumping to his feet. Her haggard hazel eyes followed those strong, beautiful hands until they rested defiantly on his hips. With that enchanting Tigres head tilted back, he broke into laughter, roaring with delight. She looked at him quizzically, not knowing what crazy-making he was up to this time. "My gracious lady awakes!" he announced flamboyantly.

"I haven't seen such showbiz flair since Barnum & Bailey," she frowned suspiciously. Ching was amusing, certainly, but what is he up to, really? Her weariness was growing; today's strained attempts to engage those youngsters were taking their toll. Resignedly, she lowered her head to the pillow. How good it felt to simply rest! "Mr. Ching, you exasperate me," she managed to say. "Please. I'm begging you. Stop all the mystery and just tell me outright why you attended my lecture today. I am, of course, completely awed by your extensive knowledge of this country's cultural pathology. But, your erudite grasp of antiquated circumstances smacks of your being something other than a Distrito loyalist. Won't you please be straight forward long enough to explain why you have engaged me today and why you are now here by my side?"

She watched his eyes twinkle warmly, as he sat himself again by her side and carefully picked up her strong, weathered hands. Wordlessly, he clasped them both in his, gently turning them upward. To her surprise, Ching then leaned down and kissed each palm solemnly. She found this a most disturbing and curious thing to do. When she raised her brows questioningly, he hastily released her hands and said, "Dear, Dear Doctor, there's so very much work to be done! You simply do not have my permission to retire!" His eyes had welled with tears.

"What nonsense!" she sniffed indignantly. "I have absolutely no intention of retiring! Surely you must know what I stand for - what my aim is, Mr. Ching. Why, I would never, ever submit without first having achieved that goal." At this, she bolted to a sitting position, and squared herself to confront him. "However, I do insist that you answer this: Why all the buffoonery in the Hall today? Why couldn't you have helped me out? Why obstruct my attempts to introduce the students to deductive reasoning?" She eased herself back against the canvas pillow and waited.

"Dearest Doctor, if you would take a moment to assess your current circumstances, you..."

"'Current circumstances?'" she echoed dully.

"Well, certainly," he gently replied. "Your Permit to Speak, for instance. You will never be issued another. You know this to be true, correct?"

"To the contrary! Why, the permit cessation has never been an obstacle. I'll simply annoy the agency until they see fit to issue me another. But, how is it you are privy to this circumstance, Ching? What of my Privacy of Information rights?" Her face instantly fell. She looked terribly gloomy, as though she already knew the answer.

"Doctor," he sighed, "our allotted time together is drawing to a close, so I will get to the point quickly. I understand all too well what it is you wish to accomplish. In my convoluted way, I was trying to get you to speed up to the crux of your message, so that everyone in the audience might benefit from hearing its rationale. Unfortunately, I only managed to eat up your precious permit time. I'm afraid the People's Hall was only a waste of our time."

"Why do you say 'our' time? I was under the impression that I, the lecturer, had a message to convey. I wasn't aware that you were there to convey one also. Mr. Ching, do tell me what your message is! Get to it, please!" She added impatiently.

"Oh, Dear Lady," he said shaking his head. "I have no message, really. I was simply debating your stance on cultural issues. You see, I understand what it is to have enjoyed a traditional family upbringing. I would have considered it an honour to join you in your discussions about the patriarchal family and how it had been the very root of our earlier culture." He pushed himself up from the cot and began pacing with agitation. "I understand only too well that the man-woman marriage was a superb institution. Actually, it was the bedrock of the strong, courageous country you once knew. You were blessed to have personally experienced what this country once knew as its traditional family structure; a structure that depended upon mutual respect and cooperation for its survival. Headed by an authoritarian father and honoured wife and mother, the paternal family unit exhibited a proven formula for the successful upbringing of obedient and well civilized children. We both understand that the primary function and responsibility of parents was to mold their children into decent, self-sufficient citizens. We know that the man-woman institution of marriage was self-perpetuating because of its empowering nature. Why, it had been celebrated and envied by the civilized world for centuries! To reflect upon that distant time feels like visiting a wondrous dream, doesn't it?" he asked.

The Doctor's pale face radiated approval. Ching was both relieved and pleased to watch as hope returned to the old woman's handsome features. He suddenly felt sheepish. "You've surmised, haven't you, that I, too, am a product of such a family?"

"Well, I've suspected as much. But, that being the case, why all the subterfuge?

"It's quite simple, really. Surely you remember Legislative Session 2027, don't you?"

"How could I forget!" she answered. "You're referring to The Turning and its series of monstrous injunctions that ultimately smashed all vestiges of individual self-determination." She felt chilled at this thought. Deeply fatigued, she reached for the faux flannel blanket and pulled it up to her chin.

He handed her a cup half filled with Sector Green. "Please sip this slowly, Doctor. It will help you regain your energy." She obeyed without protest, thinking the sustenance of her own food grown mesh would have been preferable. She understood that the overhead visual surveillance of her module made this choice impossible, so she said nothing. Actually, the tastelessness of this synthetic broth was not as objectionable as its mandated ingestion. She returned the cup to him, resigned to the reality of things; she'd never taste whole nutrients again. Her assignment to this module made that certain.

"Well, it was due to The Turning order that my family left this quadrant before I was born," he continued, placing the cup on the floor. "Father and Mother understood the projected dangers of that dehumanizing mandate. You see, they were determined to biologically conceive me, fully aware that, pursuant to LS 2027, undertaking a live birth would have been met with swift imprisonment and surgical correction."

"How fragile she looks," he thought to himself. "But, we can discuss my beginnings some other time," he said decisively. "I told you, my dear, dear Doctor, that the world today isn't ready for you. I can't imagine when it ever will be," he added softly. Today, Distrito's pervasive powers forbid your philosophy of self-determination. In your world, individuality was once something we strove for; something we idealized and praised. But, I needn't 'preach to the choir,' need I?"

He suddenly shook his head, as though relieving himself of something irritating and unwanted. "Today's People have only combined needs, and those needs are being met within each sector. In return, all The People know obedience to Distrito. They expect to be taken care of, for they have learned this is their right. Your hope that they might take individual action in any way is frivolous. Who wants to be plagued by the demands of self-imposed goal-seeking? Eh, Doctor?" he added in feeble jest.

"Anyway, as with any aberrant behavior, should someone be so foolish as to undertake unorthodox action, they know to expect Distrito's compassionate forgiveness for that 'poor judgement.' Although forgiveness is part and parcel of social justice, it is only rendered after the transgressor yields to a prolonged reinforcement process." Winking, he added sarcastically, "And you and I can attest to how effective WeCare therapy can be, can't we, Doctor!"

"I'm so tired of this nonsense. I wish he would just leave me, let me rest," she lamented weakly. She looked searchingly about the room, feeling disoriented. "Mister Ching, how long have I been here?"

~~~

"That family name was passed on to each of their products, rendering them legitimate."

XXXIII
RENEWAL

"You see, my friends, Doctor Brons has been a most valiant and tenacious leader. She now lies sequestered, approaching transition. However, for the many years she was able, how courageously she fought to reintroduce the dignities of man! How persistent she has been in her relentless battle to reinstitute our God-given right of individual action. For the Doctor to have withstood agonizing decades of institutionalized harassment has been more than inspiring. I cannot think of any other who could have borne the pain of exile and barbaric ridicule she endured. Her tireless dedication to her mission has been astonishing! Such a sight to behold," he sighed. "I am honoured to have witnessed her final presentation in The People's Hall. Regrettably, that includes watching her exquisite stamina give out and exhausted body carried away.

"Nevertheless, my dear warriors, how pleased the Doctor would be to know that you, too, were in the auditorium that day and you did, indeed, hear her call to action. I can only imagine how happy she would be to see us gathered here today!

"To quote that very lovely individual of utmost honour, 'Let's get down to the business at hand, shall we?' Who would like to summarize what we've discussed so far?" he asked. The young woman raised her hand. "Yes, 14, go ahead."

"Thank you, Sir. In our last meeting, we agreed that Doctor Brons' latest lecture was her final attempt to tell to us about the deliberate destruction of the traditional American family. In her hurry, though, she was only able to touch on a couple things. We understand now that she was hurrying because the Permit that gave approval for her to speak was the very last Distrito will allow her. Looking back, I can see why she was rushing to tell us in simple terms about some events that were anything but simple."

"Which events, 14?"

"Well, the one that really got my interest was her saying something about a 'We Fight For You' movement. I'd never heard of it before. So, until you explained to us later what that meant, I couldn't really follow what she was trying to tell us that day."

"But, now you do understand that We Fight For You consisted largely of angry females and their anger ignited the malicious malignment of all males until the masculine gender was viewed as insignificant?"

"I think so," she answered. "The Doctor tried so hard to describe a few methods used by the powers behind the movement, but she just didn't have enough time.

"Fortunately, time is in our favor tonight, so please go on."

Nodding her head thoughtfully, the brown-skinned woman continued. "The traditional family was the main thing the Doctor wanted to talk about. She wanted us to know that its healthy existence was critical to the successful survival of that good Nation. She has traced, event after event, how the family was broken up and belittled until it became a useless shell of what it had been for a very long time.

"The traditional American family was made up of a small group of people, who looked to the male as their family's authority head. 'Patriarch' is what she called him. His offspring, then called 'children,' were biologically connected by physical conception between that patriarch and a female mother. I think you told us last week that that societal structure was so strong and so good for their culture that it had been thought of as sacrosanct for some two hundred years."

"Yes! That is quite right, Sector 14!" he exclaimed. "So, in order for Distrito to take away the power the patriarch had over his family, there were a few things it had to do first. It was one of those things Doctor Brons wanted to make a point about. Do you remember was it was?" he prodded.

"I do. That," she said smilingly, "was a legal process called 'Opt Out Divorce.' It was a law made up by a group called 'congress;' a group that was paid by The People to represent them and their wishes. Of course, Distrito had congress dissolved long ago," she added parenthetically. "Anyway, because many married females at that time no longer wished to be tied down to what had been the time-honoured position of homemaker and wife, they sought legal remedy to liberate them. That remedy allowed them to shed those burdens of responsibility at will and with no questions asked."

"If you're saying," Ching said, "that prior to Opt Out Divorces, males and females married each other in order to secure an institutionalized business arrangement that was to last their lifetimes, then we must be curious enough to ask why marriage was established in the first place. Can you tell us, Mr. Waters?"

"Yeah, this part was really interesting to me, Mr. Ching. Before marriage, females didn't have laws to protect them or their offspring. A male would – if you can imagine this – implant a female with live sperm, which then produced a child. But that male had no reason to take charge of either that offspring, or the female. After his physical urges were seen to, he didn't usually stick around. This generally meant that the female, now a mother, was left alone to fend for herself and the product."

"By product, you mean, offspring?"

"Yeah. Sorry. Anyway, you told us about the really bad conditions those mothers lived under. If they were lucky enough to know the comfort of lodging, it was generally filthy, and nothing they could really call their own. Forget about getting Rewards!" he laughed nervously. "Sometimes they had no food at all. A lot of them even starved in the streets," he said shaking his head.

"And those women – why didn't they ask for help?" asked Ching.

"Well, like you said, there was no marriage and no Distrito then, so they had to actually scavenge or beg for scraps, if no one took them in. You said many of those offspring died from lack of food and shelter, and the mothers, still alone and unprotected, knew no better than to repeat the same stupid cycle."

"Quite right! Would you then say, Sector 14, that this was a good situation for the fatherless offspring?" he prodded.

"Oh, no!" she replied.

"No? Why not?"

"Well, when a male child had no father around, he had no one to teach him the ways of civil men; i.e., he was left alone to finding ways – sometimes barbaric – of simply surviving. A father could have taught him the skills of self-sufficiency, providing for himself and, eventually, his own family. Growing up without a male authority to instruct him about respectful behavior and hard work, those male children usually became their society's parasites."

"And when a female child had only a mother to watch, who lies down in return for food and a place to rest, that female child knows nothing else. As did her mother, she would assume the same degrading cycle, often producing the hapless offspring of more than several men.

"The nice part of the story," she offered, is that the patriarchal marriage could replace that awful way of life. In exchange for a vow to honour and obey, the married female was judged an authentic family member; someone worthy to share her husband's name. That family name was passed on to each of their products, rendering them legitimate. Products of unmarried females were called 'bastards' - a name for offspring considered lowly and worthless; those who were ignored and left to scratch out an existence. Lacking legitimacy, they were scorned."

"Excellent review, you two! You have brought us to the reasoning behind man-woman marriage contract. Why would a woman willingly give up her so-called freedom to become the ward of a male? And why would a man agree to legitimize his offspring with her? What was their agreement? Well, that answer is at the very core of our beloved Doctor's crusade; the crusade for individual integrity; the cause we all choose to carry on."

Seeing their anxious faces, he said, "It was a simple, but most advantageous arrangement. In return for a woman's fidelity, her husband would be certain that the children she bore during their marriage were legitimately his. This was of supreme importance to him and his forefathers, because only legitimate offspring were given the respectability of the man's family surname. Having a respected surname assured access to formal education, business opportunities, and family fortunes, all of which qualified them for creating legitimate families of their own.

"In addition to societal legitimacy for her children, marriage also provided the female – or woman - a respectable standing within their society, the comforts of a home it was her duty to maintain, and protections against the dangers of life outside legal matrimony. Understood?"

"The benefits of marriage are easy to understand, Sir. What we don't get is why did those behind We Fight For You wanted so badly to destroy it."

~~~

"Ah," he sighed, "I have never been certain about the why of it, 14. The Doctor and I have witnessed the wretchedness and destruction myopically caused by that movement.

"Of course, human beings have always consisted of decent, as well as indecent men; honest as well as dishonest; honourable, as well as not. So, I again remind you of the common pledge to our mission; to always rise to excellence."

"Doctor Brons is well known for that statement," Sector 14 offered. Actually, those were the words that woke me up. She made me want to learn about the concept. I started by searching for what excellence meant. Since I'd never heard it before, I figured it must be Old Talk. I was really scared someone might find out what I was doing and report me to Tribunal."

"Did that happen?" asked the young man?

"No! Can you believe it? So, I thought I was in real trouble when you stopped me as we were leaving The Hall and told me about these meetings. I thought you were turning me in!" she laughed lightheartedly.

"Would you say the risk has been worth your coming here?" Ching asked.

"Of sure I would. You've shown me that I have a lot to do now – so much to accomplish and that others are counting on me. Please, Mr. Ching, go on with what you were saying."

"Very well. Many times I've reminded you two that there are always exceptions to the rule, particularly when it comes to human behavior. So, please keep in mind that I am going to speak in generalities. You asked why the WFFY wanted to destroy the patriarchal family. And I can reply that it truly is a mystery that anyone who was mature and well meaning would want to tamper with anything as functionally healthy as man-woman marriages. Men honoured their wives for the homes they created and the offspring they produced. A man's home was considered his castle. He was honoured for having earned it, maintained a secure home for his family, and provided society with more productive members by way of his children.

"The true homemakers – the wives of those heads of family - were revered for providing their offspring with the formative instruction needed for their development into well-informed, well-mannered contributing members of society. As part of that formative instruction, the children were taught to be respectful of others, especially their parents, elders, and the laws of the land. In short, those children were taught first and foremost by their mothers and fathers how to be civilized members of a civilized culture. You see, those mothers fulfilled their traditional role of homemaker. It meant they stayed home to make sure it was properly maintained and the children properly cared for. The female's role had always been a full-time vocation. It had to be, because there was nothing more important than grooming offspring for their future roles as decent, productive citizens. Of course, that was the WFFY's first complaint.

"Those rabid whiners hammered the entire country about the sheer injustice of the man-woman family. They called homemaking servile and demeaning. First they cried out about married women wasting their lives; that they should hire a maid to come in to clean the house and bathe the children; that they, in order to gain self-respect, had to seek different careers – careers that would free them from needing the protection of their husbands. They…"

"That was really silly," broke in the young man, his voice shaking with conviction. "Even we can see how important mothers were to raising children. My gosh! How nice it would have been to have a mother; someone to explain things, someone to hold us… Right, 14?" he asked.

"You're understanding the situation pretty well, Mr. Waters," said Ching. But such facts did not matter. For some reason –

or reasons – the We Fight For You mob had the entire country enraged about this. Nearly everyone was shouting about female rights – as though they had somehow been stripped of them. The right to work, for example. Homemakers were hounded to leave their homemaking jobs, assured they were worthless unless they earned money outside the home. After all, with your added income," they heard, "all those demeaning, boring, repetitive tasks like housekeeping, caring for the children, ensuring they were taught about goodness and morality, were beneath them. 'Trivial' is what those responsibilities were called."

"Didn't that throw everything out of balance?" asked Sector 14. "If the female was outside of the home working, how could she still be the homemaker and make a home for the children? I mean, if she was no longer at home doing the home making, didn't that go against the marriage agreement?"

"My, my! How very proud our Dear Doctor Brons would be of you! This is where Opt Out came into play. When the women wanted to shed their responsibilities as homemakers and mothers, and breach their marriage contract with their husbands and fathers of their children, they didn't want to wait to do it legally. You see, before Distrito, around the 1970's AD, in order to get out of a marriage, a divorce was sought. That divorce would not be legally granted without good reason, or 'grounds,' to be more accurate. I believe those grounds were adultery, inability to produce children, and something else I can't recall. So, the trouble was, even if the woman could prove evidence of those breaches, getting through the process took a very long time. Also, the woman's ability to stay in their home and have financial security after the divorce was usually uncertain. That's when the Opt Out Divorce came into play. By the way, 'financial' has to do with a monetary system of exchange. We can get into that later."

"Oh, good. That monetary business is beyond me," admitted Waters. "You were saying that Opt Out was easy and there were no questions asked. Was it really that simple?"

"It was thought to be so, at first. Opt Out radically changed a family's life. Almost immediately, the man lost his home, his family, and was still compelled by the court to support his children and their mother, but without the benefits of being at home with them and sharing their life."

"Did males ever go the Opt Out way?"

"Certainly. But, because the movement was so radical and hostile toward males, even if the husband had good reason for not wanting to continue the marriage (and by good reason, I mean that the woman did not fulfill her domestic chores or wifely responsibilities), the man was still asked to leave his home, support the children, and continue supporting his irresponsible wife. The Doctor has cited cases where the women took the children away to a distant location where their father could not see or even speak with them."

"But, the court wouldn't go for that, would it?" asked 14.

"Unfortunately, it often did. There were times when the woman would take the offspring away because the father had been cruel to them, but I'm not referring to those situations. I'm pointing out to you that Opt Out divorce, along with jurists who were sympathetic to the WFFY movement, commonly ordered the separation of children from a loving parent and overtly punished men for unjust reason. The true reason was they were men. Remember, men at that time had had a very long history of wielding power over women and others less fortunate. Male power had been the governing cultural force until then."

"But, if she is the one who disregarded the marriage, it was entirely unjust that the man would be penalized for her breach of contract. The way you describe it, it seems to me that when he lost his wife and family, he lost everything he had earned with his labor; everything he had created for his family, as a whole, with nothing in return. He lost the comfort of his home, his daily contact with his children, and no homemaking or physical services by his wife. You know, that law is crazy! What really troubles me is that there were no questions asked of the woman. Their marriage contract required that she provide physical comfort to her husband. In exchange for that, he provided her with a home, food, and other needs. So, when she left and no longer gave him those services, why was he still required by law to pay for them? That was indecent, really! There were so many more injustices against men caused by women's unethical disregard for marriage vows, right?"

"That's right, added Mr. Waters. I see now why the Doctor was trying to cover the injustices of that Victimized Females Equality Act."

"Suffice it to say, much unhappiness and disillusion were caused by the WFFY. Before it enjoyed so much power, most mothers and fathers raised their offspring until they were competent adults, able to support and provide for themselves. It took a mere two generations to change that. Actually, within a few short years, our federal government (replaced by Distrito, as you know) had also made males irrelevant in other ways. Through taxation, unmarried mothers and their children became the wards of something called 'welfare.' This welfare was in the form of money, housing, and even medical care. Again, no questions were asked. Those mothers were told by the government that it would withhold that welfare if they were married to the children's fathers, so those men were asked by their women to leave the home. This gradually resulted in males and females avoiding marriage completely. Pretty awful, don't you think?" Ching asked.

"I'm thinking about the boys of those mothers. Who taught them to be fathers and husbands?" Waters asked. "Who taught them kindness, cooperation?"

"Sadly, they received no such instruction. By simply observing, they saw that woman didn't need to respect their fathers as providers, for the all-knowing, compassionate government took their place. That government ordered those children to go to schools where no real education was provided, so they ended up with no worthwhile instruction from either their fathers or the so-called educators. Rather than working to correct the cause of the problem, like overturning the Opt Out divorce and disallowing the terrible court rulings inflicted on fathers, or stopping punishing taxation of workers to support those who refused to earn it, the problem metastasized by horrific proportion."

"Mr. Ching, I've been thinking about what you said earlier about men teaching their boys to become fathers and husbands. It seems to me that, if the government replaced fathers – and sometimes mothers, too – the training needed to properly perform those roles was no longer necessary. I mean, if offspring aren't trained to do something – perform a role, then there will be no one capable of filling those roles. This had to eventually lead to those roles dying off - disappearing from society," offered Waters.

"Yes," that's exactly what happened. Not only did the societal roles die off, but the needed discipline and self-restraint of adulthood perished, as well. Dr. Brons was greatly unnerved and saddened to have watched that insidious deterioration spread year after year. 'Like a cancer,' she called it.

"So, these meetings are meant to teach us our actual history, so we have a chance to restore things," said 14.

"Yes, that's the hope. You see, unless you understand how things were, how noble and fine our nation once was, and that the cohesive force of that nation was the traditional American family, there's just no possibility of recreating it.

"You need to understand that our nuclear family structure was destroyed from within. The Doctor and I believe this was done intentionally, as its destruction was executed smoothly, one essential component after the other. A clever and effective plan, actually. And that plan also included separating elders from their families."

"What are 'elders'?" asked Sector 14.

"Good question. Well, I supposed one might think of them as very, very, old ancients. Today, they're called Remnants," Ching explained. "Long before Distrito, elders enjoyed the well-earned respect of their children and their children's offspring. They were highly revered for their expansive life experiences. Because younger members hadn't lived long enough to gather even a portion of the knowledge their elders enjoyed, no one questioned the elders' authority. To the contrary! Their sage counsel was always considered invaluable and relied upon by the younger members.

"Nevertheless, just as the nuclear family broke down, so did the extended family. The elders were no longer considered essential to the family unit, for it had been dismantled to the point of not functioning at all. No longer did elders enjoy the security of living their final years with their offspring. No longer were they shown the dignity of contribution, such as sharing household duties in return for their room and board. No longer were they asked to take part in the civilizing of the young ones. At that point in our history, civility was rarely practiced. It had become a subject of derision; an archaic concept; a silly waste of time.

"As a result, elders soon followed males into the wasteland of cultural irrelevance. As most things irrelevant, they were pushed aside, warehoused in some facility away from those they had once thought of as being family. This arrangement became the accepted thing to do; by way of physical removal, the elders were prevented from distracting the younger family members from their important busyness and recreation. That warehousing continues today. Distrito assigns compartments according to physical and mental ranking.

Seeing wide-eyed puzzlement before him, he explained, "You've heard of 'module containment,' haven't you?"

~~~

"What's the purpose, anyway?

XXXIV
SWEET RELEASE

Aly's wizened eyelids were drawn tightly. Her Rapid Eye Movement was being monitored from the adjoining room by a most impatient transition specialist. "Get on with it, Remnant! You're making me miss Rewards!" he whined with thin, unmoving lips.

According to protocol, he was to observe and record all her functions until they ceased. In the specialist's opinion, she had been on that table far too long. After all this time, he had lost hope she was ever going to die. "What's the purpose, anyway? You're so damned ancient; can't be of any use to The People at all," he thought disdainfully. It was then he saw the incoming directive:

ORDER TO ELIMINATE
DISABLE DEVIANT'S LIFE SUPPORT NOW

Ecstatic with relief, he hastily tapped the "Disable" option on the screen. "Beep!" it responded shrilly when he was already half-way across the room. "If I use the side door, I can still make afternoon Rewards!" he thought gleefully. Bounding through that portal, he imprinted his DNA and left the station. In his haste, he never looked back to see the next pop-up:

Processing Level 2 of 3

Deviant's thought activity interrupted upon initialization:

"One's dignity is reflected by the integrity of his action. It is the quality of that action and the means by which it is undertaken that constitute one's character. In order for the highest standards of integrity to prevail, every action he undertakes must be one of individual honour, guided by moral principals and sincere..."

Processing Level 3 of 3

To finalize elimination, tap *here*.

~~~

As the "tap here" flashed unattended throughout the night, Doctor Aly Brons lie dreaming. She was peeking through the lace curtains, watching her two most favorite people. They were dancing slowly. A smile crept over her little face, as she hummed,

"We just couldn't say goodbye!"

~~~

Glossary

Altruistic Law:	Regulatory requirements compelled by the BCI.
Anti-masculinity Movement:	An offshoot of the 20th Century Feminist Movement, this group repelled traditional masculine strengths and hierarchical positions.
ATT:	After The Turning. The Turning was the cataclysmic shift from US Constitutional governance to authoritarian control of Distrito in the early 21st Century. (Also see *LS 2027*, below.)
BCI:	Bureau of Caring Inclusion, a Distrito enforcement agency.
Beneficent Care Facility:	Distrito institution for implementation of Compassionate Compliance.
BTT:	Before The Turning. (Also see *ATT*, above.)

Distrito:	Autocratic governing body that seized control of the failed United States of America. (Also see *ATT*, above.)
Global Edict 1320:	Following The Turning, global directive proclaiming heterosexism a forbidden hate crime.
LS 2027:	Legislative Session of year 2027 AD. Responsible for the enactment of The Turning.
Primary Infusion:	The Peoples' first Reward session of each day. Approval to abstain from any given Primary Infusion may only be obtained through advance Sector grant.
Rewards:	Directive for regulated periods of physical and emotional satiation. (Also see *Primary Infusion*, above.)
WeCare Therapy:	Clinical correction of forbidden individual action

~~~

About the Author

Marceau O'Neill is the pen name for Patricia Birren-Wilsey.

After many years in the field of income property investments, Patricia now devotes herself to full-time writing. Previously a resident of California, she now lives in Oregon with her husband and two captivating felines.

~~~

Another Book by Marceau O'Neill:

"I Know You Know I'm Out Here!

A Contrarian's Call for Respectful Communications"

Other works by this author may be found
on www.marceauoneill.com.